RITUALISTIC MURDER – A THRILLER

A Prequel to The Kanke Killings Trilogy

KUMAR KINSHUK
KOLKATA, JULY 2021

DISCLAIMER

Book Title: Ritualistic Murder
Book Author: Kumar Kinshuk

Published by Kumar Kinshuk
Flat 1402, Tower 5, Urbana, Anandapur
Published in Kolkata, India

Printed and bound by
Smart Digital World, P-5, Scheme-VIIM, CIT Road, Kankurgachi, Kolkata - 700054

This edition 1st published in November 2021

ISBN 979-875-369-4072

Copyright © Kumar Kinshuk 2021

Kumar Kinshuk asserts the moral right to be identified as the author of this work.

This is a work of fiction. I have reorganized space and time to suit the convenience of the novel. Except for public figures, hotels, and institution names, any resemblance to persons living or dead or actual events is coincidental. The notions revealed are those of the characters. Please do not confuse them to be that of the author.

All rights reserved. No part of this publication may be reproduced, stored in, or introduced into a retrieval system, or transmitted, in any form, or by any means (electrical, mechanical, photocopying, recording or otherwise) without the prior written permission of the author. Any person who does any unauthorised act in relation to this publication may be liable to criminal prosecution and civil claims for damages.

DOWNLOAD A FREE EBOOK NOW

Download a free cozy mystery short story with women sleuths - **The Husband of the Siren** by clicking on the book cover below:

You can check out my Amazon page and check the various books that have either been published or are under a pre-order. The three published works are **Two Indian Girls, Fatal Belief** and **Daybreak**. The book in your hand, **Ritualistic Murder**, is a prequel to this Trilogy and one can read it even as a singular work of fiction, in the thriller genre.

Thanks for having Ritualistic Murder in your library. May I request you to share your review of the title in Amazon, Goodreads and BookBub? This gesture will be wonderful as it helps the author get more books out there and to get quality work for you in the future.

TO

My Dearest Brother

Kumar Gaurav

He read my manuscript many more times than me and helped me declutter myself to pursue this tough project. It is because of his relentless follow-ups and pertinent inputs that this manuscript is complete.

It would be good to mention, I completed this manuscript on the 19th of July 2021, which is Gaurav's birthday. Many happy returns of the day, Gaurav!

ACKNOWLEDGEMENTS

Wish to thank all my readers who took out time from their busy schedules and for reading my earlier books. It has pushed me to write further. It means a lot to any author, more so to a new author.

I get a few fan mails now, and I am happy to have created a list for myself. I wish to work with perseverance and with a sense of passion, to create better work and to chisel my art with every upcoming book.

I dedicate this book to my readers and to those who have read the entire trilogy, Two Indian Girls, Fatal Belief and Daybreak. You give me the conviction to perform, and I take it as a cue to dish out better work in the future.

This book was basically curated to get you to peek into the illustrious background of the police officer. All of you have liked Inspector Rajiv by now, so this book was necessitated to show why, in the first place, he became a celebrated cop in his area of work.

CHARACTERS

1. Ravi Yadav — Sales Manager – IT – ITCON Limited
2. Radha Singh – Manager - Consumer Durable Sales – Pukar Group
3. Raman Singh – Radha's father & Businessman
4. Chitra Singh – Radha's mother & Homemaker
5. Suraj Singh – Radha's elder brother & Businessman
6. Puja Singh – Suraj's wife & Receptionist at a Beauty Parlour
7. Saurav Asthana – Wealth Management Relationship Manager – Godavari Securities
8. Raj S. Shetty – Proprietor – Shetty Electronics
9. Mr. Murali – caretaker at PG
10. Akshay Shastri – College friend of Radha
11. Kamal Shastri – Akshay's father
12. Reema Shastri – Akshay's mother
13. Rajiv Kumar - Police Inspector
14. Pradeep – Police Constable
15. Shamsher – Police driver
16. Raka – Police ASI (Asst. Sub Inspector)
17. Bholu Ram – STD Booth owner
18. Dr. M. Tiru – Professor of Anthropology
19. Rajveer Singh – Saurav's father-in-law
20. Guruji – Cult chief

CHAPTERS

Contents

DISCLAIMER 2
DOWNLOAD A FREE EBOOK NOW 3
TO 5
ACKNOWLEDGEMENTS 6
CHARACTERS 7
CHAPTERS 8
INTRODUCTION 12
   12 November 2021: 21:00 Hrs 12
CHAPTER 1 14
   18 January 2010: 21:00 Hrs 14
CHAPTER 2 27
   19 January 2010: 19:30 Hrs 27
CHAPTER 3 33
   18 February 2010: 21:00 Hrs 33
CHAPTER 4 38
   20 February 2009: 21:00 Hrs 38

CHAPTER 5	40
22 February 2009: 12:30 Hrs	40
CHAPTER 6	47
22 February 2009: 17:00 Hrs	47
CHAPTER 7	52
22 March 2009: 17:00 Hrs	52
CHAPTER 8	57
19 February 2010: 11:00 Hrs	57
CHAPTER 9	63
19 February 2010: 12:30 Hrs	63
CHAPTER 10	66
19 February 2010: 19:00 Hrs	66
CHAPTER 11	72
20 February 2010: 11:00 Hrs	72
CHAPTER 12	78
21 February 2010: 13:00 Hrs	78
CHAPTER 13	85
22 February 2010: 13:00 Hrs	85
CHAPTER 14	88
12 April 2009: 17:00 Hrs (9 months back)	88
CHAPTER 15	92
18 April 2009: 11:00 Hrs	92
CHAPTER 16	97
27 February 2010: 13:00 Hrs (Present day)	97
CHAPTER 17	102

18 APRIL 2009: 21:30 Hrs (10 months back) 102
CHAPTER 18 106
04 March 2010: 11:30 Hrs (Present day) 106
CHAPTER 19 110
05 March 2010: 19:30 Hrs 110
CHAPTER 20 112
22 July 2009: 19:30 Hrs (8 months back) 112
CHAPTER 21 117
31 December 2009: 19:30 Hrs (Three months back) 117
CHAPTER 22 120
8 MARCH 2010: 11:30 Hrs 120
CHAPTER 23 125
9 MARCH & 11 March 2010: 14:30 Hrs 125
CHAPTER 24 131
17 February 2010: 06:00 Hrs (Just before the crime–one month back) 131
CHAPTER 25 139
12 MARCH 2010: 11:30 Hrs 139
CHAPTER 26 153
13 March 2010: 13:00 Hrs 153
CHAPTER 27 156
13 March 2010: 15:00 Hrs (Same day) 156
CHAPTER 28 163
14 March 2010: 14:00 Hrs 163
CHAPTER 29 170

15 March 2010: 15:00 Hrs	170
CHAPTER 30	174
16 March 2010: 15:00 Hrs	174
CHAPTER 31	188
17 March 2010: 03:00 Hrs	188
CHAPTER 32	193
19 March 2010: 13:00 Hrs & 20 March 11:00 Hrs	193
EPILOGUE	209
28 May 2010: 13:00 Hrs	209
LET'S CONNECT	213
15 November 2021	213

INTRODUCTION

12 November 2021: 21:00 Hrs

This novel, Ritualistic Murder, is a thriller, and it is a full work. The author created this novel to establish a character arc for the protagonist, Inspector Rajiv. In further works in The Kanke Killings Trilogy, we showed it as a fact that Rajiv was the best in business, in the police force of Jharkhand and Bihar states. I therefore created this novel to establish his credentials as a detective. This novel establishes, beyond any reasonable doubt, why people refer to him as the best detective in the police force of the two large states of India.

Whilst this story is more of a thriller, one can read it as a prequel to The Kanke Killings Trilogy, which includes Two Indian Girls, Fatal Belief and Daybreak. These three books are more of murder mystery novels and therefore, are slightly different in their pacing from a thriller, like Ritualistic Murder.

The four books establish Rajiv unequivocally as a super detective in the department, but as any protagonist, he has had his hours of grief and terror. How we fight our horrors daily, make us who we become.

Book 1 of the Trilogy, Two Indian Girls, is a full book wherein Rajiv has a major role to play. In Book 2 of the Trilogy, Fatal Belief, the author has shown another intelligent detective as a protagonist. Rajiv does not have much of a role there, but Vishal, a senior detective, does an awesome work. Book 3, Daybreak, has a sort of mixing of worlds of Books 1 and Book 2 and Inspector Rajiv comes back with a bang.

So, as a reader, you might just read Ritualistic Murder as a single thriller novel and quit. Nothing would give more pain to the author than that, but that is a reader's call. One can read Book 2, Two Indian Girls, as a single novel again. However, it is better to read Books 2 and 3 only after reading both this book and Two Indian Girls. To get a flavor of the authors' mystery world, you must read the complete trilogy.

So, what are you waiting for? Just dive in here!

CHAPTER 1

18 January 2010: 21:00 Hrs

'Take cover, guys! Let us all rush towards the left side of the road. The road height from the ground will give us a semblance of protection. Raka, call for help. Let our boss know we are under fire. We do not have enough ammunitions to keep these crooks away for over half an hour. Do not spray bullets as we do not have enough of them, and they know that. They have caught us napping here, well, almost. We were driving through seemingly their territory, without backup.'

'Inspector, sir, I have informed our superintendent, and he says he is sending the backup teams within half an hour. We must keep these guys at bay till then. We have a couple of grenades, but I think we left them in the jeep, while rushing out to safety. Should I get it now? Please cover me.'

'No Raka. You all are my responsibility. We had taken a trip that was bound to end badly. We are on our own, as we did not even ask for a backup team in these areas at this hour. How many Maoists do you see in the attacking party?'

'If I read it correctly, which I assume I do, they are at least six people. There is a constant flow of bullets from at least three directions. I assume there will be at least two people in each direction.'

'Raka, guess work will get us killed. Let me get the grenades from our jeep. I assume they do not have their rockets; else they would have taken out the jeep by now. It would have been up in flames. I need cover, so now spray bullets in all three directions.'

I jumped towards the jeep like an athlete in an Olympics game.

I was about to pull the dashboard open, but I heard a rocket fired towards me, so I ran back to safety in the nick of time. I had to jump off the road surface, towards the lower-lying land, and I landed on my palms and knees. The jump to safety got me badly bruised, but I was in no mood to let go the initiative I thought I had wrested from the opponent.

'Sir, now they know whatever we had in the jeep, that is perhaps gone, and it left us to whatever we could carry out with us while jumping off the jeep. They will see an opportunity and press the pedal towards arresting us. We are sitting ducks over here. Should we begin our backward journey into the bushes?'

'No, Raka. This is a mind game for the next ten minutes. Just contact the back-up team and get their coordinates. We cannot run away. They know these locales better than us. They will find us and abduct us. We would have done a major harm to our polity, and we would have handed the Maoists a chance to negotiate hard with the government. We are government servants, and we need to protect ourselves better. Do not worry. We must just keep at it, without giving them any indications of any kind of loss. While they know we have lost our jeep, they will become restive, as they know we would have called for backup. They will run away from here soon. Losing our jeep is nothing great tactically, as this gunfight would never convert into a car chase. Yes, having a grenade or two would have helped, but it is no challenge.'

I was on a brief trip to Ranchi. I like Ranchi as it still has the good things of a small town, while being the capital city of Jharkhand State. They lodged me in the police department's guest house. My senior is not using my skills in the best manner possible. I am more a detective than a normal beat officer. He gives me cases related to Maoist related insurgencies and killings. Those are open and shut cases and the entire government machinery is aware of the issue. They are working on it politically, economically, and socially through multiple agencies, including NGOs. I have little to do in such cases. I wish to work on other crimes, including murders in our district, that are in cold blood and, of course, wish to use my studies better.

I was driving back down to the base of my operations at Latehar district. It is a small town in Jharkhand, and I am the Police Inspector in the local thana (police station). I feel it is a thankless job. Whatever I might do to protect the locals from Maoists, they do not have faith in the system. They perhaps still believe in their old ways of justice. They have faith in the Munda-Manki (Munda is a local tribe and Manki is the village headman) way of justice, that got approved in 1837 by the Britishers in Chaibasa area, and we still know it as the Wilkinson Rule. The government of India has passed no legislation in independent India to abrogate the Wilkinson Rule. They still follow the law in the local areas in the Kolhan regions, and they are possibly effective till date. Now, however, the locals or the Maoists do not believe in any rule of law. They believe in the rule of guns.

I have a driver who was sitting beside me, and I have two gunmen with me. We were going through the sinuous routes. I have a case related appearance in a local court tomorrow, hence this risk of driving back at night. We got ambushed. Latehar has been disturbed by the communist violence and in 2009, they abducted 10 Hindalco staff members for ransom. Police later rescued them. I had an old jeep, but now I will get a Gypsy. It has better headlights, and it is easy to drive.

There have been no further bullets from all the three directions. It has been over five minutes. Either they have exhausted their supply, or they have just gone back running to their dens. They must have realized any moment our backup will arrive. I had to be perceptive, and I had to hold on to my guts. I had to keep my team safe.

'Raka, just change over your direction and keep looking in the bushes behind us. I dislike this quiet. They are better equipped, and they know the terrain well. We are vulnerable. Only our bravado and our deep understanding of the criminal minds can save us. Let us also shift slightly to our left, by at least a hundred metres. Keep a watch on either side, guys. Keep sharp.'

'Sir, we have a situation. The backup team was on its way, but there has been a major accident near Latehar. They have got stuck there. They are doing their best to get out of it and move, but it will take them a precious thirty minutes more. Maoists will soon realize we do not have help and they will, likely, strike back.'

'That is bad news, but I appreciate your deduction. You are a quick learner. Let us move further ahead. They will get foxed if they were to come to our known location. That would give us only a slight edge, as they will be unnerved. They will, however, figure out soon. How many bullets do we have on us?'

'Sir, I think we will have 40 odd bullets. We will have to do man-to-man marking and take them out. We also have our small daggers if it comes to hand-to-hand combat.' Pradeep said.

'Pradeep and Raka, we will have to remember our police training. Hand-to-hand combat is as important as any other form of combat. Pradeep, the academy trained you well in hand-to-hand combat. Raka had just passed somehow. Driver Shamsher will have to help us if it boils down to that. Shamsher, hope you have done some training?'

'Sir, I cannot say I am ninja trained, but I have a brown belt in karate. That was while I was a fourteen-year-old. I have not kept myself in much of a practice, but I know a trick-or-two.'

'We should use our combined strength and tactical advantage to the best use. These guys know their jungles like none other, and this is their home terrain. Maoists are excellent in jungle combat, and they have their advantage. They will have more rounds of firepower and more local knowledge. They will ambush us at a location or time of their advantage. Their time-based advantage is getting neutralized. Let us start our stopwatch for 25 minutes. We must stay alive for this period and not get taken. Hopefully, our backup would arrive by then. So, guys, keep looking and use all five senses, taste, smell, sight, touch, and hearing power. For example, the smell of gasoline on fire is ebbing. That means we have put some distance behind us. What else do we know people?'

'Sir, I think we are getting close to a river. It might be a stream or a fall nearby. We have absolutely no idea what we have in store for us there. Can we use our google maps to figure?' Pradeep asked.

'That is quite perceptive of you, Pradeep. I can hear water near us. Let us wait as it might be a large open area and our jungle cover will go before we realize it. We are away from our initial location and let us wait in this area. Pradeep, you go up this tree and keep looking in all directions. Be a chameleon and disappear.'

'Okay sir! How do we communicate?' Raka asked.

'Use one hoot for danger and two hoots if you have neutralized it. Also, if you get ambushed by over one opponent, cry out your worst fears. We will be there in no time.' Rajiv commanded.

'Where should I wait, sir?' Raka asked.

'You keep away from us, maybe fifty metres, but be clever. They will use their maximum firepower this time around. Call out in need. Be merciless. Kill to live! That would be all.' Saying thus, Rajiv and driver Shamsher took their positions, looking in the opposite directions.

21 minutes to go.

Pradeep felt a movement in the bushes 50 metres away. He looked in the direction like his life depended on it. Pradeep looked intently. He could see a slight movement as though bushes were moving towards him. He could see at least three to four bushes moving, and he blew one soft hoot.

I replied. I knew my guys were up and awake. It was our first combat in this kind of situation, and we had started under prepared to take on the enemy. I have to bring out the best in the team, to overpower and get past the enemy over the next twenty minutes. I can see terror writ large on Shamsher's face. He is perspiring in this intense cold weather. He is also calling out his Gods, it seems, while praying on a loop through slow and consistent chants to please the Gods. I know these situations make a or break a man. It is my moment, and I will make the most of it. I will take my team out of danger and get past the post. So, Rajiv, you need to concentrate. Raka seems to be far away. He has not called out yet. He might not even have heard our hoots. So, the three of us are on our own as of now. Pradeep will be the last to get into any combat. He cannot even fire from up there as he would receive maximum firepower aimed at him. He will just drop dead. I must use him only as an eye into the movements. Only Shamsher and I have to fight the opponents, whatever be their numbers. I cannot hear or smell or see anything different yet. We have eighteen minutes to go.

'Sir, I heard something. I think they are fast approaching our location. It is like an army and it is not one or two people. It seems they are at least four or five of them. They will have enough firepower to take us down. We do not have any chance of survival.' Shamsher mentioned.

'Shamsher, how many times have you been in this kind of situation?' I asked.

'Never, sir. I am a driver, for God's sake. What can I do?'

'You are not an ordinary driver, Shamsher. You are a brown belt and a police jeep driver. Do not forget, you know every single move that any of us knows. You will stay back till it is a distant combat. You will monitor me and our team members. In a physical combat, you must jump in and help me. Together, we can take down five of them. You are my trophy here, man — don't worry!'

'If you say so, sir. I believe in you, and I know you are a well-trained officer. You are tactically sound, and you can see any situation through. I am there with you, at your command, and now raring to go.'

'That's the spirit, my friend. The game is not over till it is over. There is always a way back and we can always crawl back into the game, even at the last moment when we lose all. Never forget it. Winners are those who keep striving to do their best, come what may. Let us fall to the ground and try to hear their moves.'

I got down to the ground and put my ear on the surface to decipher any movement, and I felt the troupe was still away by fifty metres. I felt it was over five of them. My handgun had about twelve rounds. .22 bullets. They were fast, and they hit with full force. I removed my silencer. I needed the maximum impact power. One bullet for one person. That was the game. I could not waste any bullets.

Shamsher was looking in the other direction. He had a heightened sense of smell. We depended on him for smelling good food. He loved mutton and other non-vegetarian food. He could sniff the good from the bad.

'Sir, they are near us now. I think they are carrying petrol or diesel with them. They may just use it to create fire around us. That will immediately get all of us visible and we will lose our advantage, if any. Even Pradeep will have to get down for a combat. He cannot stay up the tree for long. He will be in the line of fire, literally.'

'Oh God! We did not think of that. You slowly go towards Pradeep and ask him to get down. Keep yourself perched as close to the ground as possible, never above more than half a metre. Leave me here. I will initially pick up a fight with them. You guys later cover me from behind, giving us an advantage. Now, go!'

I think these guys have stopped. There is no movement. I cannot feel a thing within the next fifty metres vicinity. They are strategizing. The attack will soon ensue.

Let me look deep. A night vision gun would have worked wonders for us. Even our night goggles would have helped. We came thoroughly under-prepared. Only I am to blame for that. Let me use my resourcefulness to the best of my ability. Let me launch a pebble toward these guys. For a moment they will get unnerved, feeling we have encircled them. It would give us time to launch an attack later. I hope the back-up team is near us. All our mobiles are now in silent mode. Even if they call us, we cannot answer. They will have to find us from near the wreckage of our burning jeep. They would have to hear us fight and come quickly behind to help. I hope Raka covers me once he hears the sounds. Sixteen minutes to go.

This is the best I could have done. I think the pebble has landed behind the enemy. Let me look by raising myself by just about a foot from the ground. I can see some movement there. Yes, I was correct in my assessment. There are five to six of them and they are now visible as they have taken their positions and I think other than one of them looking towards me, the others are looking behind. This is my opportunity. Bang! Bang! Bang!

Three of them have fallen on the ground. They may or may not be dead, but they would be immobile for a bit. I am taking a barrage of bullets coming my way. They are waiting to see whether I fire or someone from our team fires. They will take only a minute to realize we are playing guerrilla warfare. We are man-marking while they are spraying bullets randomly. They will move towards me soon. I just hope Shamsher and Pradeep are getting behind the enemy. God only knows what my ASI Raka is doing.

They are now crawling towards me. I guess there are three of them moving in my direction. We have grounded the other two or three for a bit, or they are dead. I need to concentrate on taking out these three guys. They are wearing proper assault gear like a helmet and a proper body armor. I will have to aim at their feet or at their face. No use aiming at their helmets. I hope my gun practice helps me with my targets. I see some commotion. The enemy looks rattled. They have abandoned their positions and they are rising. They are under fire from behind. I think Raka is behind them. Oh, I see one of them running to his right, away from us, towards the river. I cannot let this guy run past us. The other two Maoists are engaging Raka and Shamsher. I need to go after this third guy. Let me run towards him.

My bruised knees are not helping. I am not running at my hundred percent. This guy is creating a distance between us. I cannot hear any more rounds of fire. While we have neutralized the better part of this threat, they might even have run away, taking advantage of the surrounding darkness. I can now barely see this guy. In fact, I cannot see anyone at all. I can hear the river and I can see the trees clearing up. I will be visible, so I need to rush for cover. Oh, I cannot breathe. This guy is bigger than me and he is holding me from behind. My throat is in his grip. He has a big palm. I have to think of something to throw him off balance. His grip is tightening around my neck.

I am losing consciousness. There is no help around. I have to open his grip and break his fingers one by one. That is the only way I will survive. He can take a lot of pain in his stomach and chest and that effort is going in vain. Yes, I have broken his little finger. He is in pain and is now shouting, but he is still not releasing me. I have only seconds left now. I have now broken his ring finger and the middle finger. His grip is loosening around me. I think he is in an excruciating pain. This is my chance. I suddenly move from under his arm and turn around. I kick him hard in his groin. He is crying in pain and I might have neutralized him, but only for a moment. Bang! Bang! This big man is dead. I can barely breathe. My training has helped me save myself. There was no other way of getting out of his grip. He was at least two hundred fifty pounds and a six-footer.

'Sir, how are you? We hope you are safe. We see you have taken care of this big man and I am happy to tell you, we have taken down the other two guys. The three of us have made doubly sure the first three are back in hell. Let us pull these guys towards the road. Our backup team must be arriving.' Raka said. Pradeep and Shamsher also felt relieved.

'I can barely speak. I need a minute. My breathing is still ragged. It boiled down to hand-to-hand combat. He caught my throat from behind. At his weight and height, only my training saved me. I can hear the sirens. Let us get up towards the road.' I spoke in a shaking voice.

I can see at least twenty policemen and CRPF (Central Reserve Police Force) agents around us. There is an ambulance and two police trucks. We are getting our basic first aid. I am relieved my team is safe, and we have taken down at least six guerrillas in their terrain. All my guys have learned from this combat. We have picked up the bodies and their gear and ammunitions. They had big rifles and automatic pistols. Their stuff is better than our stuff. Possibly, our training is better. Tomorrow is another day and I have to attend the court at 11 am. There is a missed call an hour back from Diya. Will call her once we get on the road, back to Latehar. We had a date tomorrow. Just hope she is not postponing it and not canceling it. I need someone in my life now.

CHAPTER 2

19 January 2010: 19:30 Hrs

'Diya, I had a near death experience yesterday. Thankful to God that he not only saved me and my team from yesterday's dastardly attack, but also helped us in bringing those crooks to justice. My boss is happy. I might finally get a couple of suitable cases now. Have been wanting to get into investigative cases. I am done with these Maoist related policing.'

'You are a rising star, Rajiv. All TV channels have covered your bravado throughout the day. Your SP also took credit for your and your team's training. Hopefully, you would soon get what you always wanted. By the way, what is the man behind Rajiv-the Inspector? What are you like, Rajiv, as in what kind of person are you? What are your likes and dislikes and what do you look for in a companion? See, I am well past my age for having those love at first sight reactions. You are a handsome man, no doubt about it. One can keep looking at your dark black eyes and get lost in a different world. Your height, what, you must be five feet ten inches, right?' Diya asked.

'You are absolutely correct about my height. I see you are perceptive. You have an eye for detail and I might or might not agree with your description of my eyes, though. I feel it looks dull and empty.'

'Not at all. Your eyes have a depth, and they invite the person having conversation with you. Your eyes invite the other person to explore you. Well, and I am not saying any of this so that I become a constant factor in your life. I talk straight and I say what I like. I also say what I dislike. For example, I dislike our waiter has not brought our soup yet. I am freezing. It is cold today, almost like freezing!'

'Here comes your soup, Diya. I will settle for a small drink. Rum goes well in this kind of weather. In fact, you might have liked to have some brandy. It helps keep warm.'

'Jeez! I am not into drinking. In fact, I dislike people drinking a lot and then not being able to control themselves. In the police force, I guess, drinking is normal. But you must take care of not over-drinking. That impairs your ability to react to negative stimuli.'

'By Joe, negative stimuli and all! Are you a biology student, by any chance?'

'Nope! I graduated from the Humanities stream, and have read Psychology, Sociology and Political Science. We can happily talk about those subjects. Everyone studies biology till Standard X you see!'

'Yes, I know. The way you put it; It blew me away for a moment. We do not get to meet many intelligent people in our lives, though. We meet thugs and muggers and dacoits and murderers. Our life is also interesting, but only if we are passionate about our jobs. Otherwise, it is too difficult a job, and it taxes the person and destroys his life. I, for one, love my job. What about you? Are you working somewhere?'

'I know. You love your job. You've been, what, only a year into your job, right? How can you be so sure?'

'I know because this is what I wanted to become through my impressionable age. What about you?'

'That's great. You love your job, and you must also love your life partner. Else, never get hitched. Times are changing. Honestly, let me tell you, you have no right to destroy your spouse's life, if you do not love her or him?' Saying thus, Diya winked, and she bit her red lips, which were glowing with a shining lipstick.

I feel a tingling sensation in my body and I can almost feel her lips in my mind now. I think she likes me, but I need to be sure. She is good. Quite the modern woman types. Haven't seen such babes in Latehar, of all places.

'What are you thinking, Inspector? Did I just say something unnerving, aka modern woman of India, in the rural heartlands of Jharkhand? How on earth?'

Diya smiled an electric smile. She had a tiny dimple on her left cheek. She was fair, and she was tall for an Indian, at almost five feet seven. Diya could be a Miss India participant for all I knew. She was confident in her skin and while she wore a salwar kurta and dupatta, she could wear any western attire with elan.

'Why are you blushing, Inspector? Did you pick up any wrong hints? I was just asking. And I think you are talking to yourself while I am speaking to you. It seems the entire role reversal here, as in my asking the questions here, has unnerved and upset your calculations. You are taking it slowly, chewing your feelings about me already. Do not rush to any conclusions. You know nothing about me.'

'No, I am not rushing with any feelings or emotions or judgment or theories or calculations about you as of now. That does happen, but not so soon. Being in my service, I am well trained on that aspect and for a modern woman like you, I will need a lot more information to base any judgments on you. Look, it can happen two ways, going ahead. We go the local way, as in getting to know each other slowly and over sometime, propose to each other. We make our judgments about each other over that period and take a studied call. The other way is the India in a hurry way, or youth in a hurry way. Let's just go to my place tonight. We will explore ourselves together. If we like enough of each other over a relationship of a few months, having explored ourselves in every way, we go steady and eventually get married. I am game for either way, but I would prefer the second way. I do not wish to waste my youth over apprehensions and pretenses and I wish to take it on.'

'You are a man in a tearing hurry, Inspector. And why not? You just got a lease of life. Who knows? Why waste one's time to experience things in life? Have you experienced many such women in the past and haven't got steadied with anyone?'

'You are right. A near death situation changes one's perspectives in life. I wish to take things fast. Can't wait now. I haven't said or done anything like this in the past to anyone. I haven't been in any kind of relationship earlier. What about you?'

'That is difficult to comprehend! Are you a virgin? Ha ha ha… what a role reversal here!'

Diya laughed out loud. Other people in the restaurant looked towards us. I felt a little twitchy. It was a first for me and while I always felt confident in my way of handling people; she was the more experienced one. I did not even want to ask her about her past, but I was okay and I wanted to have a go on her present. I had to respond fast; else she might again think she had rattled me. It was going well for her. She had revealed she was not from Latehar. She was born and bred somewhere else, possibly in Mumbai or Delhi or even abroad.

'Diya, I think let us go out from here. We can go to my place. I will order some dinner and we can have some scotch.'

'I would like that.'

She winked again. We got up. I kept five hundred bucks on the table, told the waiter, and went out. I could not wait anymore. My excitement knew no bounds. I had my new Gypsy in the parking. She had her car parked as well. I told my driver to take my Gypsy. I got into her car. She drove me home and within ten odd minutes; we were at my residence. On our way, I had ordered for a chicken pizza.

She went to my washroom. I took the pizza delivery. She had taken a quick bath, and she was wearing my bathrobe. She sat next to me. I felt overjoyed at the prospect of enjoying the evening. This was unthinkable in Latehar, or anywhere in Jharkhand and Bihar. This was the new India we used to talk about in a hush-hush manner. I was there for the experience, and I did not want to judge her or myself. We ate a couple of bites and started kissing. My hands started exploring her. She responded well. And we had a quickie right there on my sofa. It was some experience. We finished our pizza and watched some Indie songs, the horny ones. We then went to my bedroom.

It was a night to remember. She went away at 2 am. It worried me as my town was not safe for women at that hour. She was confident of taking care of herself. I did not know her well enough. She had bowled me over and I did not wish to know anymore. I was on her speaker phone while she drove to her place. I bade her 'night night,' and I was already waiting to meet her.

I remember little of that night, but I was late to my police station that morning. I felt I had under-slept, and I had that look when Pradeep and Raka came over to me with a query on their faces. I confided in them. They were happy for me, and it was a lovely time. I was looking forward to meeting my boss, as a man now. I had done well professionally and personally. I was a changed man, with more experience and with better insights into my own life. I wanted to speak to my boss and ask for a deductive case as an opportunity to explore my learnings. I knew he will not say no. I had to wrest any new upcoming case as an opportunity to prove my worth. Simultaneously, I hoped there should not be any crime in the city. And God, I knew I would get a quick opportunity!

CHAPTER 3

18 February 2010: 21:00 Hrs

Radha's body was found lying in a lane in Netarhat, also known as the Queen of Chhota Nagpur hills. Netarhat is a village in the Latehar district of the Jharkhand State in India. Netarhat was a popular hill station during the British times.

My boss called me and handed over the case himself. I did not have to ask for it. I was a changed man, and he had faith in my abilities. It was a relationship I wished to foster, and I was happy I got an opportunity again to make a difference. I had to use my deduction skills to the best of my abilities to get under the killer in or killers, in this case. I reached the site along with Radha's family members. Radha's family members traveled from Ranchi while I traveled from Latehar. Radha's parents and other family members were howling, and they wanted to hug her body. They wanted to touch her physical being. The policemen had covered her thoroughly bruised, cut and naked body with a white cloth. She had bled a thousand cuts. I did not allow any family member to go near the dead body. Police officials who went about collecting any proofs at the site surrounded her body.

The entire process looked mechanical to the family members and to the local crowd. The residents of the area got enraged and astounded. This had been the first such murder in their hitherto peaceful environs.

Netarhat has had seen the worst of the Naxalite movement, but they have seen no disturbance in their daily lives or that of its tourists or in the lives of the students of Netarhat Residential School. This school is famous for chart topping results from its students in the erstwhile Bihar and now Jharkhand Board exams. The school attracts the most committed teachers and the brightest students who live and learn in a Gurukul environment.

There was a stunned silence that winter night. An ambulance arranged by my team members took Radha's body away. We sent her body to the nearest government hospital for a post-mortem. Raka and Pradeep were on site, and they had marked the location with yellow tapes. Policemen took multiple photographs of the dead body and of the room in which they found the body lying. They took away any potential evidence that they could find in the area, including her purse that was empty of her belongings and her clothes. The gold chain that she used to wear regularly was missing. We combed the entire area, and my team members collected any potential evidence in police evidence boxes.

I spoke to the family members consoling them and telling them to meet me after a couple of days at my police station in Latehar.

'Raman ji, Chitra ji, I feel extremely sorry for your insuperable loss. I feel overwhelmed and equally dejected and lost. Netarhat has been a peaceful village and, by the looks of the body, it looks like rape and murder. The criminals have taken her belongings. However, strangely, it doesn't look like a purely rape, loot, and murder case, what with the beads and sharp cuts at various points in the body. I am sorry for referring to Radha as a body.

The criminals subjected her to agony and relentless pain. I know she was a career girl, and that she was doing well in her job at Bangalore. Believe you me, I have received multiple calls from Mumbai and Bangalore, from her office and from the owner of Pukar Group. I would do a thorough investigation and get to the depths of this murder. This event disturbs the tourism potential of this area, and our government has taken this rape and murder investigation seriously. I will head this investigation.

'Inspector Rajiv, we want to do the last rites. God takes the best people early. She was our world, and it is now demolished. She was a genuinely kind soul, and she was very dear to her extended family, friends, and colleagues alike. When can we collect her from the hospital?' Raman cried.

'Don't worry Raman ji. I would keep you informed. I have your coordinates. By the way, are you going to Latehar or are you planning to stay at Netarhat itself for the next two days?' Rajiv asked.

'Inspector saheb, we are going to stay at the same hotel as Radha was staying over the last couple of days. We have got ourselves a booking there. The hotel owners feel hurt and angered to hear about the incident, and they have been most courteous to manage the booking for the four of us. Do you have any news about Akshay? He was her boyfriend, and they were here together.'

'Akshay Shastri is missing. His belongings are still there in the hotel. I went and checked it out myself. It opens up the case literally and figuratively. We have no clue as to his whereabouts. What came unto him? Was he kidnapped? Was he murdered as well? In that case, we should find his body soon. My men are doing a thorough search of this area with the help of the local villagers. The villagers know their territory well. We are using almost twenty men, as we speak, for the search. I would advise you to go to the hotel now, and I am also going for the search. I am here at Netarhat tomorrow as well. We need to figure out what happened to Akshay. His parents are restive, and they are coming here tomorrow.' Rajiv mentioned.

'Oh, it is so sad! We were not in favor of their traveling to this place alone. We had told her to give us a few days and we would all have come together. However, young children, you know, they are all powerful and they want to experience everything by themselves. This trip was their pre-marriage trip. I should not have allowed them this liberty. It is all my fault!' Raman cried out loud.

I asked Chitra ji and her son Suraj and daughter-in-law, Pooja, to take care of Raman. I went towards the deep woods. I had a couple of policemen with me, and all of us could talk to one another on a walkie talkie. The cellphone signal dimmed in the interiors of the jungle. The jungle had a multitude of animals, including leopards. Villagers had seen lions and tigers as these jungles were close to the Betla forest.

I called out the search as we could not collect any clue in our three hours of deep, multi-directional search. I scheduled the search again for the next morning. I wanted to speak to the hotel manager and find out if they were aware of anything that may help.

The hotel manager was back in his quarters, but he saw me because of the urgency of the case. He mentioned he was totally unaware and that he had checked with the staff at the hotel. None of them were aware of Radha's plans for that day. He, however, promised to get back to me if he found anything that might be helpful in our investigations.

I spent an uncomfortable night in the same hotel, eager to understand the case. I had a call with Diya, and we missed each other's company. I did not want to keep up all night, so I closed the call soon and tried dozing off around 2 am.

CHAPTER 4

20 February 2009: 21:00 Hrs

I am time. I move the world and the universe according to my wishes. I keep the time for people and for all living beings. I am the one who controls people's lives and their movement. I control people's thoughts and the way they would lead into their future. I control whether someone would have a good time or a bad time at that instant of their lives and I am the only constant in anyone's life. I am time! With every movement of a second, I change the way people live and react to external stimuli or to their internal thoughts. I control their actions and their words. I am time.

I control the global narrative. I control what happens in the world. I control why the world is in a recession or how it turns towards a growth phase. I control people, their minds, and their possessions. I control whether someone would live or die. I might sound like God herself, but I think of myself as that moving second. I am that moving minute and that moving hour. Some worlds work slower than the other worlds. People in villages work slower than their counterparts in cities, and people in metros like Mumbai or Paris work around the clock. People in a remote village like Bundu in Jharkhand possibly work casually. All of them are under my control. I define how they live their lives and I control their lives completely.

I am narrating the life of Inspector Rajiv and the surrounding people. No one knows them better than me. I have mapped every second of theirs. I exactly know how their lives would pan out and play out over the years. I am the one controlling them. Sometimes I feel people are so anxious about such minor issues in their lives and they keep fighting matters that would eventually not impact their lives. They forget their longer-term approach and their vision. They keep bogged down by small little irritants in their lives.

I would keep you all in the loop through my narration. I would keep you glued on, and I would control the narrative from here. In fact, I have always controlled the narrative. I would continue to do so. I allow Inspector Rajiv to talk to you directly in first person.

I am time, and I am the narrator.

You and I can always have a direct chat. I could give you glimpses into other people's lives. I could show a peek into your own life. That would have to wait for now. Let me do my job as an author here and you must read on. You must be true to yourself as an expert reader of fiction. We would meet again soon.

CHAPTER 5

22 February 2009: 12:30 Hrs

'Radha, long time! How have you been?' Akshay Shastri hugged Radha with a big smile on his face. Akshay looked amiable and sharp. He was similar in height to Radha, and he had a decent physique. He must have been doing his daily jogging. He was a fitness enthusiast, and he was verbose. Akshay was likeable but more of a brother material. He had many friends during his college days, including Radha, but none of them had a serious relationship with him.

Everyone liked Akshay, but he used to remain in his own make-believe world. He would spend time with everyone, smiling and taking part in debates and discussions. However, he did not take any sides, and he used to be someone who would end up being on the right side of the powerful people. Radha thought he lacked his opinion and, therefore, his personality. However, she liked him for what he was. A good buddy. Period. Things might have changed over the years, post college. Therefore, she wanted to give it a chance. One date would not harm, she felt.

'I am good Akshay. You are like your namesake actor. Likeable, lovable and everyone's friend. Have you ever taken cudgels in your life, buddy?' Radha crashed Akshay's party. She wanted to see a different side to his personality. She wanted to see if he had ever taken a stand against anything yet in his life. Job might have changed his methods and his outlook on life. She wished to see that fire under his belly. She wanted to see how he reacted to negative stimuli in a direct confrontation.

'Radha, you completely surprised me there. You were not like this, were you? I thought we were always good together in college. Has something changed? Why are you so aggressive?'

'Gentleman, I just wanted to check whether you continue to be so gentle in your approach; or that life might have changed you. Job rush and career changes things and changes people. College life is different. Life is different. Do you remember our professors talking about the ravages of life and the importance of split-second decision making? I have seen it happen in real life. I used to joke about these utterances of our professors, saying they just wish to psyche us. No, they were correct. I have seen the best and the worst of people responding in different ways. Have you seen it too? It is of an academic interest to me.' Radha summarized her thought and put it forth succinctly.

'Radha, I am impressed. You impressed me with your attitude and your overall learning mentality earlier. However, you are sharp, incisive, and analytical. Life has changed you for the better and you are a powerful person. I like this quality in you. As far as your question is concerned, I relate to it and I have seen people in that mode; reacting to external stimuli in varying methods. I guess I am not the same as well. However, nothing would change me for my friends from school and college. I continue to be the same old likeable and lovable person. Yes, I did not like taking cudgels amongst friends in the past and whilst obviously everyone has his or her own opinion on topics and subjects, I was happy just to mention mine. I never pushed people to accepting my viewpoint. That was me. That summarizes me today also as far as dear friends and family go. So, the way I would react to your verbal diarrhea on a topic would differ from the way I would react in my office. With my colleagues, I need to play it smart. I need to push the boundaries and push the envelope to gain the advantage. I get done in sometimes, but at other times, I come out trumps. However, I still dislike politicking, and I do not understand it either. I cannot even claim to understand politicking.

In an organizational setup, it affects my growth potential. I might be an easy prey. Let that be so. I do not intend to change way too much. I intend to continue the path of a healthy approach to life and to business. I might lose a promotion or two in my career, but I would be a fortunate man. I would not have changed myself for the worse and I might still be happy. Eventually, all of it evens out and what some people might achieve in a few years, others might achieve later. One should never compare one's life with others. Everyone has a different trajectory of growth. One would never know what someone might have done to achieve something superlative. He might have had to take bitter pills in real life.' Akshay put it beautifully for Radha to chew on and consider.

'You have a point there, Akshay. I am slightly different. I am a go-getter and I just power ahead, even if that meant trampling over jobs and people. I have learned it the hard way whilst someone tried to crush me while I was still a trainee. I took the fight to the finish eventually and got some of the choicest dealer accounts. I cannot see colleagues trample over me now. I do not get into anyone's domain, but I do not allow people in my domain to influence. I wish to create a dent in my market through hard work and relationships that I create. I wish to use my education and I wish to create a good life for myself.' Radha said.

'You were no different, Radha. You were always a go-getter, and you always had that clarity in your mind. You are an achiever, and you would always remain one. My only submission is, take your time and grow healthily. Have a good life beyond office and enjoy every bit.' Akshay said.

'I see your point here, Akshay. Don't you worry, I have a glorious life outside my office, and I have my two friends who take care of me. They are my PG mates, and we are thick as no one's business.' Radha said.

'I am happy, Radha. Friends are possibly the only people who keep people going over the long term. Deep relationships are often healthy and keep people sane in bad times as well. May I know who they are and what do they do?'

'Well, they are sweet. Ravi is an IT Sales Manager in a good firm, and he is doing very well for himself. He is a perfect guy, and he is very much like me. He is also a go-getter, and he keeps pushing the limits. He is also very sorted in relationship matters and he is a wonderful coach. Saurav is a great guy. He is thoughtful and lovable. I feel he is diffident and does not take some tough calls in life. However, he is everything that one would want to have in a life-partner.' Radha let out her emotions.

'I see Saurav quite enamored you. Is he more than a friend?' Akshay asked.

'No, not yet, be he could be. I do not know it myself. I kind of like him, but I am not sure. He is someone who might never take a lead and I am someone who might have taken a lead, but I need some time to evaluate and come to an agreement with my feelings.' Radha said.

'Oh, then I guess I do not have any chance. Do I?' Akshay asked with an inquisitive and humble face.

'Ha ha Akshay! That is a nice way to check. I give that much to you. Akshay, I do not know. I take time in my decision making. I do not even know that I would be correct, eventually. However, I have my methods and you need to keep trying, I guess.' Radha said in a hushed tone, looking actively at Akshay with a slight smirk on her face.

'You beat me there, Radha. Are your parents not after you to get married? My parents are very much after me now. It is difficult to stay single, I guess.'

'Did you not have any flings yet, Akshay?'

'No Radha. I did not get time and never had the energy, I guess, to seek dates. Have been on a couple of such dates with colleagues, but things did not work out. I have also been busy in my work and wished to settle down before getting into any life-changing events. However, I feel I am none the wiser! Hands up!' Akshay answered.

'I see. I understand what you are saying, Akshay. I have also not had time and time has just flown past us. It is already seven years post college, but we have not settled in our lives or in our careers. This changed global environment is doing no good either.'

'I agree with you, Radha. In my banking industry, things have gone haywire. We still have our jobs, but anything could go wrong. Biggest of the global banks are failing and it seems it could now happen in India too. We are under great stress. Banks are under intense pressure from the regulatory bodies, and we have immense sales pressure. Oh, let's forget about all of this. How are your parents and your family? Have you spoken to any of our college mates recently?'

'Akshay, this is my first meeting with a college friend, out of college in these seven years. I did not get in touch with any college mate, and I would say I never tried it. The problem is all mine. Now, however, we should meet up more often and keep in touch. The bigger the circle gets, the better it would be.

'I agree with you, Radha. We should get a few more friends involved, and we should relax. Hope you liked the food here?'

'The food was sumptuous, and I loved having taken this time out to meet you. It was lovely to interact after a long time. Let me pay half the bill.'

'No issues there, Radha. I know you are a modern, independent woman and you would have your way. The bill was not much, anyway. I have deep respect for you, Radha, and I like you. I hope we would meet again.'

'Of course, Akshay. We would meet again. We can also chat when we cannot meet. It would be nice.'

'Can I drop you to your PG, Radha?'

'No, Akshay, I am going somewhere else. I have my car. I drive myself. Thank you for your time today and keep in touch!

'Absolutely! It was great meeting you after such a long time. Would catch up again, soonest! See you. Bye!'

They went their ways. Radha was happy to have met Akshay. She did not have any feelings for him yet. She wanted to give him some space and some time to herself before she could meet again. Radha wanted to explore and evaluate if the slightest of option existed, of getting steady with Akshay. She wanted to wait and see if she liked him enough and if she could marry him. To cut a long story short, I can tell you, as time and as the narrator, that she would have to work hard on her own feelings to figure her relationships out. She would have to think it through and take positive steps to take a decision that she could stay with, for life.

CHAPTER 6

22 February 2009: 17:00 Hrs

'How was your date, Radha?' Saurav asked.

'Why are you being so inquisitive, Saurav?' Ravi looked askance and asked.

'Just like that. Wanted to know if she enjoyed her lunch. Do you mind sharing it, Radha?' Saurav was visibly unhappy at Ravi's banter.

'Why would I mind, Saurav? Ravi, I too did not understand why you asked that question.' Radha said.

'There is a reason I asked, Radha. Anyway, you guys would not understand. I would also like to hear about your date Radha, as both of us had a boring afternoon. Nothing to do really and we just watched an action movie apart from having our home cooked lunch. Neither of us wanted to go out today. You were not there, you see!' Ravi had a wicked smile on his face.

'Ravi, you are naughty! Ok, I had a decent outing and a wonderful date. Do not know if it was technically a date, but I had a good time meeting an old college friend. He is a genuinely good guy, and I loved spending some time with him after such a long time. Akshay was a good friend in college as well. He is sweet and good-looking. However, he is not a typical cut-throat competitor. I should say he never was a cut-throat competitor. He was a cheerful guy to have around oneself and he was someone who would never pick up a fight. I cannot say that he was docile or something, but he was someone who would never take cudgels with someone. It was not his style. Akshay is charming and stylish minus the oomph quotient. He is sexy and good looking, minus the killer instinct. He was good at teamwork and presentations, minus the fire in the belly kind of guy.'

'Oh God! You had him mapped completely. Were you guys seeing each other?' Saurav asked, rather perplexed.

'No Saurav. I cannot say we were not seeing each other as we were in the same team for all project submissions, etc. but we were not seeing each other like couples; if that was what you meant. I have always liked him for his overall personality and stuff, but I also had this issue with him for not going the distance if it came to be protecting oneself or to be fighting for one's rights. He was a happy-go-lucky kind of friend who would be around you. He was helpful, and he was a decent student. Akshay was also someone who could take a lot of shit because of friendship, and he would not bat an eyelid. He was a total sport and an enormous support for all the teammates. I liked him quite a lot. Somehow, we never spoke once we were out of our colleges. Only the day before, he called me out of nowhere, asking if we could meet up. I now totally understand why he would have called for this meeting.' Radha took a deep breath and kept mum for a moment longer than Saurav or Ravi would have liked.

'Do not give me these weird looks, guys. He obviously wants to get into a steady relationship with me. He likes me and he said that he always liked me, earlier as well. Over the last four years, he has had given it a deeper thought, and he believes we would make a good couple. He also believes we were made for each other.' While talking, Radha was looking away from Saurav, but she was now and then checking on his facial expressions.

'Yes, and he is under pressure now from his family members, including his parents. They have asked him to get married soon. I told him that my parents also want me to get married as I am already twenty-eight. Oh! Did I just utter my age? Don't worry, it is only you guys here.'

'Okay, so what is the outcome of the meeting? Have you guys agreed to see each other like couples now?' Saurav was inquisitive and somewhat defensive. Radha could easily make out that he did not like the conversation as it was going till now. She could also see that Ravi was enjoying the conversation and that he could understand Saurav's discomfort.

'Saurav, be patient! All of it cannot work out in a single meeting. You know fully that I take these things somewhat slowly. Who knows, someone else might be in love with me already and I am not aware?' She smiled at Saurav and saw him in his eyes for more than what Saurav could take. Saurav flinched and looked towards the clear sky outside.

'Radha, I guess you could be correct in taking things slowly. Give it sometime, maybe a month. Then think about meeting this new date of yours. I sense someone already loves you enough but is not coming out with his emotions yet. It might just be that circumstances are not allowing that person to be upfront about it. Give sometime to it and things would take shape. Hope I am correct, Saurav?'

'Of course! I should think these things through before taking calls. These are life-changing decisions, and one must allocate enough time to it. One should try to read others and then take a decision. Hasty decisions do not help anyone, I guess.' Saurav opined.

'I agree, Saurav and I would wait for that slow decision maker to come around and take a call on his life.' Radha said.

'Radha, do not wait for over a month. You are already twenty-eight. You must get steady with someone good. How does it matter if he doesn't have the requisite fire in the belly? I know for a fact that the fire that you have burning inside you, for work of course, would provide enough fuel to your boyfriend as well. So, take my wiser counsel and take a decision over the next month!' Ravi said.

'Let us see how things shape up from here!' Radha said, and all of them sipped their coffee.

Mr. Murali had gone out to get some provisions, and he should be back anytime. The three of them went out for a couple of hours and get back by dinner. They could just walk in the nearby nature park. Everyone knew the filth in the air, and it became a media noise from time to time, but nothing came out of it.

CHAPTER 7

22 March 2009: 17:00 Hrs

'Guys, I am going out on my date. Yes, it is a date. The first time I met Akshay, I was not sure. This time I am,' saying thus, Radha looked askance to Saurav.

Saurav had been quiet an entire month, processing the information about his career and about his personal life. He must have thought it through, and he did not speak out openly to Radha or to Ravi. Radha knew he was the silent types when it came to deciding and that he would trust himself and no one else. Radha had lost her patience. She was on the wrong side of twenties and every day that she waited; it did not help her. Radha had a decision to take about her life. She liked Saurav for what he was. It included his ability to take a hard look at his life and keep his secrets to himself.

Saurav knew he had lost Radha to time and not to anyone else. If only she could wait a few months and he would be good to let her know how much he loved her. He did not want to go down on his knees and get betrothed while he was jobless. He knew he would get a job soon, but he knew Radha did not have all that time in her life for him. She needed a quick answer, and he was not capable of delivering at that instant. Ravi had counseled him to speak up, but to no avail. Saurav will let it pass, as he felt the time was not right for him.

Radha met Akshay that evening, and she felt delighted. Akshay had come prepared for the evening. He took her out to an expensive restaurant where they dined in luxury. Thereafter, he guided her to a nightclub, and he showed her his elements on the dance floor. He was a nifty dancer and his charm bowled her over. He was a salsa specialist and Radha did not know about it.

His rhythmic movements under the psychedelic lights guided Radha's steps in a manner she never imagined. She was not the dancer types; she was a go-getter and a fierce fighter in her domain. Radha allowed herself to be taken over by the man in motion. The crowd thoroughly enjoyed Akshay's soft but mesmerizing dance moves off and on the floor. They made way for the two of them and Radha knew she was getting into something that would change her for life.

After a couple of dance numbers, Akshay guided her back to the booze counter. Radha got shaken and stirred, literally. She needed a moment, and she went to a nearby powder room. Having had a couple of drinks and a few shots, Radha felt dizzy. Akshay guided her to his car and carefully took her to her PG.

Saurav opened the door, and it was 2 am. Akshay got Radha inside the house. It surprised Saurav for a brief while, but he soon recovered and took over Radha to guide her to her room. He tucked her in her bed.

While he was laying Radha on the bed and tucking her, his t-shirt went up, showing his bare back for a moment. Akshay could see some strange undulations on his skin in the exposed area on the back. He felt puzzled, but did not broach the topic with Saurav.

Saurav closed Radha's room behind him and looked towards Akshay. Saurav had a lot of questions in his mind, but he decided not to ask. All Akshay said was Radha was wasted after a few shots of tequila and he wondered if she has ever had tequila.

'Thanks for dropping her home, Akshay, am I right?' Saurav asked.

'Yes, and you would be Ravi or Saurav.' Akshay murmured softly.

'I am Saurav. Ravi is fast asleep. He has a big day tomorrow. Good to meet you. Sincerely hope she was a sport, and she did not trouble you. Well, I am sorry I see her having put you through so much already. You would have lost the last left hint of tequila in your body. May I offer you something, like a small peg of whiskey for the road?' Saurav chuckled.

'Thanks, Saurav! Some other day. And absolutely no problem there with Radha. She is a total sport. I have known her for ages as a good friend. I, however, intend to know her now as a future wife. I know you two are her guardians in the city and you guys take great care of her. All her talks center on you guys. After a point, I asked her if she were having an affection for you, Saurav. I am not lying here.' Akshay mentioned, looked towards Saurav briefly and walked out of the house.

Saurav bolted the door and went to his room. He was restive, and he did not get a tidy sleep.

He was wide awake the whole night, thinking about Akshay and Radha, thinking about himself, and thinking about what life would be without Radha. He knew he was deeply in love with Radha, and he was allowing her to walk away from himself, like sands of time.

Radha had a terrible headache the next afternoon while she woke up. She had missed going to her office. She had multiple missed calls from her clients and from her boss. Radha had a missed call from Akshay. She decided she would call them back after a while. Saurav was ready with his magic potion for headache. Radha gulped it down and thanked Saurav for being there for her.

Saurav guided her to the dining area and got her seated on a chair. She could see lovely lilies in front of her. Akshay had sent it to her that morning. He blew her off her feet with this gesture once again. Last she knew, she was swooning at Akshay's fluidic dance moves. Well, it was time to get involved. She knew Saurav was good for her, but she found the unpredictability of Akshay a bit of the X-factor. Saurav suddenly looked an also-ran.

Saurav felt the same while talking to Radha. One evening had changed the equation. It would require an effort to keep Radha to himself. He had lost an opportunity while it was there. Saurav was not a personality type (p-type) that would take a loss for real, easily. His p-type dictated he would get in the dugout and fight. Saurav's instincts were telling him to fight off the bad influence of Akshay and get Radha home. He did not like what he heard about Akshay's dancing skills or the expensive restaurant or anything about last evening.

Was it for real? He thought to himself. He knew Akshay was handsome, but he knew he too was handsome, of a different kind, and he fully well knew Radha liked his personality over Akshay's. She had mentioned Akshay's personality as someone who would never get into a fight. He would only share his opinion, but he would never labor to get it across to others. He knew Radha liked his own fighting fit personality, and he had a better physique with all the workouts that he did. Now, however, Akshay had blown her off her feet. He had to plan his next moves if he had to remain in the battle somehow.

Radha took a longish bath to get over her hangover. She liked her date with Akshay, and she wanted to narrate all of it to Ravi and Saurav. She knew Saurav might not like what she had to say, but she felt he had brought it upon himself. While she did not want to judge Saurav, she did not want to take away her own fun because of him. If he felt bad or felt pathetic, he was responsible. As her friend, however, he must listen to her exploits. She wished to take the afternoon easy and wait for the evening. She planned to narrate every bit of information to her two best friends.

CHAPTER 8

19 February 2010: 11:00 Hrs

I felt agitated, and I gave a mouthful to Pradeep. He was hell-bent on taking care of my tea and breakfast, whilst I had no clues about the disappearance of Akshay or even about the murder of Radha.

Akshay's parents would be at Netarhat any minute now, while the search teams were reporting a complete disaster. We could not get any clues at all, as though Akshay had just disappeared from the face of the earth. There was no blood, no ragged cloth, nothing anywhere. Until then, Akshay's parents had received no ransom calls. I was restless. Till the post-mortem report came in, I will not have much to go after. It might be better to get back to my thana at Latehar and pursue any leads there. I could always remain in touch with all the people connected to the case.

Before going to Latehar, though, he thought he would have a chat with the two families independently. He could get some information that might be useful. He had already taken the magistrate's approval for tapping the phones of all the family members of either family. Any leads from any phone calls were welcome.

Kamal and Reema, Akshay's parents had arrived, and they were dazed with travel and this terrible news of a missing son and a deceased yet-to-be-daughter-in-law. They had gone to meet Raman and family and they were all together, taking the sad news slowly. Their lives had gone topsy-turvy, and it would never be the same.

In their hearts, Kamal and Reema still believed that their son was out there, somewhere, and that he would soon connect. Villagers were calling this entire case *'The Mystery of the Runaway Boyfriend.'*

It was harsh on Kamal and Reema because they knew their son and they were clear in their head that their son would not run away from such a situation. It was, therefore, that they feared the worst. Either, God forbid, those goons might have killed him, or they might have kidnapped him, and they expected a ransom call, sooner than later.

I met the two families again. It was lunchtime, so all of them had a listless lunch. None of them enjoyed having food, for once. In some other setting, the way they had planned everything, including the engagement ceremony and the wedding, they would all have loved to have food of the most garish varieties. It was not to be, sadly!

Post lunch, I met Akshay's parents. They sat on the verandah of the hotel, and I fired my first volley.

'Kamal ji, tell me something about Akshay. What type of person is he? Can he do such a ghastly act? Can he kill his fiancée?' Rajiv asked.

'Rajiv ji, I thought you wanted to tell us you have some clues about the whereabouts of our son. I am surprised that you are painting him as the culprit here! Why on earth do police always go after the wrong guys, wasting a lot of extremely important time? Why do you guys always feel that a husband would have killed his wife or that a lover would kill his beloved? They were on cloud nine, having accepted each other. They were making wedding plans. We had, as parents, approved their wedding, even though we are from completely different backgrounds and different castes.

Both kids were good people, and they were doing very well in their careers. I would request you to search for relevant clues. From what I have heard, this murder looks like no other. It seems, the local religious practices and rituals could have been a cause.' Kamal mentioned with half contempt.

'Kamal ji, let me rephrase my question. I do not blame you or your opinion here, as you are his father and you have lost your son's fiancée. I want to know what kind of person your son is like. Kindly map him for me.'

'Rajiv ji, Akshay is our dream, and I don't know of a better person, as he is an honest, caring and sharing son. He is not opinionated, and he does not get into any fights. Akshay was never into picking up fights at his school or even at his college. He would not pick up fights, even on different subjects of discussion. Akshay would let people know his opinion on any subject, but he would not expect them to change their views or opinions because he had a different view. He is full of life and a sweetheart. You could not dislike him. He is a handsome and charming young man. We were after him for his marriage and we were giving him dates so that he would either find someone or he would allow us to get him a dutiful housewife. We felt thrilled to hear that he had found Radha. She was a sweet girl, attractive, and modern. Radha was great at her work, and she had a positive attitude toward life. She always wanted Akshay to take a stand on issues, but he was happy the way he was or the way he is.'

'Ok, so what was their program overall? Had he come to Ranchi recently to meet Radha and her parents? Were you also planning to get over to Ranchi, to formalize the wedding?' Rajiv enquired.

'Yes, Radha wanted Akshay to meet her parents. He took our permission to go to Ranchi. We allowed it and we were also secretly planning to visit Ranchi within a couple of days, to meet Radha's parents and to ask for their daughter's hand for our son. Our world had changed for the better, and we went ballistic. We informed our sides of the family of an impending engagement ceremony. It could have happened a few days from now. I had spoken to Radha's best friends, Saurav and Ravi. Both would have joined us in a couple of days. While we plan our moves, we are simply unaware of His moves and His plans for us. Our world, as we know it, has changed and I will tell you that my son is not a *bhagoda* (someone who runs away from tough situations). He can never be a runaway boyfriend. He would not run away, come what may. His instinct would have been to protect his girlfriend. We do not know what befell, but I am certain my son is out there, fighting for his life as well.

You must be quick. Do something, please. Get us our son and get us a closing on the case. We want to know what happened to Radha and why did it happen. We want to know who did it and why? That would be an important closure for Radha's family members as well. This incident has numbed and dazed them. It is not good for them or for us. Please do something about it, Inspector Rajiv, and keep us informed.' Kamal pleaded.

I spoke to them for a while and left; after having comforted them, I would do my best to find Akshay. For me, Akshay was the killer or the prime witness. In either case, it was pertinent to find him and get the killer to justice.

I feel I am a no-nonsense cop and recently I have got enough media attention. I have gained some reputation and people feel I would be good at cracking such tough cases. It is therefore imperative that I do my best, and that is my promise to my society and to my city.

A local peasant came running to me and handed me an important clue. It was a shirt that was smeared with blood. The villager took me and my team to the location where he saw the shirt that he picked up earlier. It was just below the huts in a secluded area. It was an old, dilapidated hut, which was not in use, and its occupants had moved to an improved house. He found the shirt just outside the dilapidated hut.

Police combed the area, and I instructed our dog squad members to take a tour of the area. The evidence collection team was on the job already. They searched the hut and its surroundings for the smallest of evidence and fingerprints. We left nothing to chance. It was a mammoth exercise, and I was looking for further clues. I was looking for a breakthrough.

CHAPTER 9

19 February 2010: 12:30 Hrs

I was silently going around the dilapidated hut. What I saw in front of me confused me. There were many earthen pots that were colored by urn, roli (a mixture of turmeric and lime powder used in auspicious occasions to decorate colorfully) and sandal. They had used the place within the last twenty-four hours. The earthen pots were all broken by an impact of a sharp object. That had littered its holdings on to the earthen floor. The liquids would have disappeared, but the earth was dark colored at places. It was difficult to decipher the contents, but it included uncooked rice, doob (strands of grass) and a lot of flowers that had gone dry. They might have used a weapon like a sword or something similar for a clean impact to break the pots. The room was not large, but it could have accommodated six to eight people if they were to sit tightly. I had an eerie feeling that it was dark magic, and they have sacrificed the girl. It might have been for a good omen or for any other weird thought or belief.

I muttered to myself that I needed to meet the Panchayat Pradhan (Village Chief) and get an understanding of their local rituals. I was now concerned about Akshay, and I had a feeling that Akshay's parents might not get any ransom calls. They might have sacrificed him as well. In that case, however, we must find his dead body. If the villagers had done what I thought they had done, why were they helping the police? Was it the work of a particular sect that still believed in these archaic traditions and beliefs? Whatever be the belief, I was doubly sure we would find Akshay's body. I told my team to double up the manpower and diligently comb the entire area.

For a moment, my mind veered towards thinking if it could be the handiwork of an animal. But I soon recovered and removed that thought from my mind as I did not see any feral like marks on Radha's body. She had sharp cuts, possibly done by controlled movements of a razor blade or a sharp, small, and thin knife. Those marks on the body were fresh and she would have received it whilst she was in an intense pain, over the last twenty-four hours only. It was all getting clear to me. It increasingly convinced me that the murder was a sacrifice by some traditional tribes in deference to their Gods, and it was to achieve a higher purpose. It perplexed me to think of such tribes and such thoughts in my own dynamic country.

I asked my men to send the latest evidence to the backend team at Latehar and to ask them to study it carefully. I went to meet the village chief soon thereafter.

The village chief felt the murder was not a handiwork of anyone from their village. It was a gory act and his village folks desisted from black magic. In fact, they had an internal code against black magic, and they used to hand out open punishments to people practising the same. The village chief reiterated it was a handiwork of external people. It could be tribesmen, or it could be anyone else but not his village folks. According to the chief, his village folks believed in modern education because of a school of international repute in their village. Their kids might not have been students at the school, but they went through decent education themselves, and they were very supportive of visitors and students in their village. They knew it was a source of income in their lean months and it was, therefore, welcome. I got a fresh perspective, and I thought to myself I should not be rushing towards a solution. This was a case fraught with risks and I had to be careful before casting doubts openly on anyone. I had to tread carefully, and I had to use his deductive gray matter to the core.

I went to meet Radha's parents thereafter. I told them that my team was doing its job, and that I had employed over forty men at the search party. I was confident of cracking the case. I told them some crooked villagers who might believe in black magic may have caught the kids. I also told them I had not reached a conclusion and with every new information, the case was getting wide open. I told Radha's parents to get to Latehar the next afternoon and collect Radha's dead body. I knew that her post-mortem would be complete within a couple of hours, and I would get the initial information soon thereafter.

I went back to Latehar the same evening, and he went straight to the hospital to check out the post-mortem report.

CHAPTER 10

19 February 2010: 19:00 Hrs

'Hello doctor!' I smiled at the post-mortem specialist in the only government hospital in Latehar.

'You are a man in a hurry, I see! Let me tell you something, Rajiv. I am stunned at the ferocity and the ugliness of the killer in this case. It stumps me that we have such people amidst us today. I was naïve to think that I have seen it all, as I have over thirty years' experience now. The severity of the crime gets compounded because the killer has used her body to perform some pujas or rites or black magic by giving her a hundred and eight sharp cuts. She has bled from every such cut on her body. So, they gave the cuts while she was alive. I did not find any suppressant in her body. She would have bled to death slowly, but she got killed by an impact of a sharp object like a knife that was sharp on either side; on her chest.'

'If I understand you correctly, you say it could be a murder for carrying out a ritual. How can you be so specific?'

'Well, I am not assuming things here. While I have no way to get into the criminal minds, I can say what I can decipher from the body. Here, we found ghee (clarified butter) on her body. They must have literally applied it all over her naked body. They also smeared her body with roli, flowers, doob (type of grass) and other items used during auspicious occasions during a puja (prayer). So, while she was still alive, they prepared her body for this ritual. They also raped her. We have found semen inside her. While most such killings happen because of an urge for sex and rape, this one is slightly different. The killer was not there for an aggrandizement of the base sexual kinds. He was after something bigger in his limited worldview. It might have been for power of the ritualistic kind, but he might have found it difficult not to give into his carnal desires. They applied ghee all over her body, including over her private parts. I understand they raped her first, then they prepared her body for the unholy ceremony, by applying ghee and other auspicious items. Having smeared the holy potion or whatever you might call it, they tied her to a bed using all her four limbs. Her arms and her legs got stretched apart, but not with significant force. She might have been in that position till her death and the timeline could be about two odd hours. After the priest or whoever killed her, they dumped her body. They did not waste time after the murder. I have nothing else to say, Inspector!' The doctor surmised.

I have nothing to ask, at least at this hour. I am dumbfounded. I could not believe it was a ritual-based murder, or was it? I could not give in to the temptation so easily. Who are the players? Why was

Akshay's body not found? What if the perpetrators did not catch him? Why did he not try to help Radha? If he was outclassed, outsmarted, and outgunned, why did he not run back to the hotel? Is he one perpetrator of the crime? Is he involved in the crime? Only time would tell. I have no choice other than waiting for complete feedback on all the evidence collected from our crime lab. I knew I will have a better understanding of the case the next day, as I will have some more information to process.

The traffic police have reverted. They have not seen any suspicious activity across all the major roads around Netarhat or Latehar. Police checkpoints got activated ever since the news of the murder came in, but there has been no sighting and no reports of any untoward incident in the last twelve hours. Typical cases of drunk driving got reported.

I had a peg of whiskey at the house. I stay alone in a small government quarter. Mine is a tough life in a small town. I had lost my parents early and I do not have anyone else in his family. I am single, but I am not available. I have Diya now in my life. I want to create a name for myself as an incorruptible and an honest policeman. I knew it was not easy when almost everyone around me depended on the other income. I wish to be known as the finest detective that Bihar or Jharkhand Police have ever produced.

I knew the next day would be a long day, and I wanted to take it easy. I thought to myself I would exercise my deductive skills once I have all available information. I feel tired due to two days of continuous work and stress. I have reported the facts that I have collated till now to my superior and I have asked him to take care of the press. I do not wish to speak to the press. I have asked my superior to hold the information of the ritualistic practices on Radha.

I felt I had a duty to protect the citizens of this country from such malicious criminals. I did not want to take up any other case till such time as I solved this case. I knew I had to go beyond the call of duty to figure out this case, as it was unique and it tarnished the reputation of an entire person. I told my superior about allowing me sometime with this case and not to allocate any other work to me. As this case was important for the government of the day, he readily agreed. I thought it fit to visit Bangalore, the place of Radha's work, and meet her colleagues and her friends. That would give me a perspective and clarify some of my doubts. Who knows, I might get some hints as well, the likelihood of which was low. I knew I had to up my game if I had to play this game.

I had no one to speak to at this unworldly hour. Diya had not contacted me these couple of days. She was aware I was handling this case, and I was busy. Every man needs company, right? I have had enough whiskey for the evening. I would normally speak to myself and analyze the situation as it unfolds in front of me. The more I speak to myself, the better I would be at demystifying the clutter in my brain. The exercise provides me with oft needed clarity and I would get pearls of wisdom by thinking through some of my earlier cases. I was supposedly a talented student of criminal minds, and I have read the biggest and the brightest of criminal psychologists. My cerebellum shows I am done for the evening, and I will fall if I continue walking, even within the confines of my home. I do not want Diya to see me in this condition. I cannot speak to her tonight. Let me be alone. It is painful to think about the premature death of my parents. I will never get over their loss. Whenever I am alone, I grieve even today, even after all these years. So, let me just doze off into the night. I need to be fighting fit for another long day. I feel this case is one such case that could destroy me forever as a detective. Boy, I love the challenge, and I would take it head on!

Tring, Tring! Tring Tring!

Is that my home phone? Why is it ringing at these hours?

'Hello?'

'Hi Rajiv, I could not reach your mobile, so I called you on this phone. Thought you must have been busy, so I called up late. Hope you were not asleep!'

'Hi Diya, so happy to hear your voice. I was going to doze off at any moment. It has been a very hectic couple of days.'

'I am so happy for you. You got what you wished for. A case. I am so sorry for the girl who saw this extremely painful death. I am happy you have got this case and I hope, and I pray, you will crack this case. It will be good for you, but it will provide closure to the families involved and the harshest possible punishment to the perpetrators of this grave injustice.'

'Do you know, Diya, you are my lady luck? You came into my life, and I have got this big case to handle.

With you beside me, I will crack it and get justice for everyone.'

'Awww, you are so sweet, Inspector! Do you want to play some Police and dacoit games tonight?'

'Do you mean you can come over to my place, like at midnight? Is it even safe?'

'I think let us leave it for today and I know you will have a big day tomorrow. Your voice is already giving me hints of enough alcohol for a day. You need some sleep, Inspector. We can always play our games tomorrow night.'

'That would be super. We can catch a bit early tomorrow and spend some jolly good time together. What were you doing?'

'Oh, nothing. I would have also slept off, but I wished to have a chat with you, even if, for a minute or two. I know you are under extreme pressure, but I could vent your pressure and give you a nice evening.'

'Dear darling, I know you can release my pressure, by exercising your writ over my body's various pressure points and pleasure points. You are creative in that department, and I totally adore you for that. Let us meet up tomorrow evening. I will call you and we will catch up. Alternatively, you could just come to my house and relax. It would be great to have you home while I get back from work.'

'Done. I will call you tomorrow evening, and we will coordinate. Night-night, inspector!'

'Good night, Madam!'

CHAPTER 11

20 February 2010: 11:00 Hrs

'Guys, do we have any feedback from our lab yet?' I asked the constables on duty at my office. One of them came to me with a sealed envelope. I took it and went into the small chamber. I had a whiteboard in my chamber, and I would scribble the day's work over it.

I looked carefully at the report. It was a lab report for the various evidence collected from the crime scene.

The report mentioned that there were three people present in the room apart from the girl. There were traces of semen found near Radha's body, but it was not of multiple people. It involved only one person in the girl's rape. Also, as per the DNA reports, they could not identify the three people as they were not there in the police database. There was one woman and two men in the room, apart from the victim. There was a lot of blood on the floor, and it was not all the victim's. One suspect had cancer, and she was at least sixty years old. The two males were around thirty years old. The two males were in good physical health. Interestingly, the blood on the shirt differed from the samples from the hut. So, it meant it was of a fourth person, other than the deceased. That was all in the report.

I was donning my thinking hat. Who could be those three people? Were they mother and sons? Were they a mother and a son while the third guy could be Akshay? What happened to Akshay? Whose shirt was that? Why was so much blood spilled while we have only one body? Where have the other four people disappeared? Are there caves somewhere in the depths of the jungle? Should I ask for helicopter help? Would I even get one on requisition? While I was deep in my thoughts, a constable came to inform that Radha's and Akshay's parents had come over. I asked him to get them seated in the conference room and serve them tea and biscuits and tell them I would be there in a moment.

'It is good that all of you are here today. We have some recent evidence. I would want someone from Akshay's family to go for a DNA test. We have found some drops of blood there in the same hut as of the victim and it would be good to know if Akshay was present there. Also, I cannot tell you much, but you can take Radha's body from the hospital for last rites. The post-mortem report is available with me, and it would be helpful to analyze the case in its entirety in the future.

Look, I am extremely sorry to say this, but it is a complicated case. The local police have solved a few cases tricky cases in the past, but this one sits perched at the top in terms of its complexity. I am doing my bit. I would request all of you to go back to your locations once the DNA test gets done. Keep in touch with me once every few days and I would keep you informed about the developments. I also wanted to go to Bangalore, once, to meet her friends. I wanted to meet at least her flat-mates.'

'Rajiv ji, I would speak to Ravi and Saurav and check with them an opportue time for you to meet them at Bangalore. I guess that would suffice for now?' Raman asked.

'Yes, let me know. Can you speak to one of them right away, please?' Rajiv insisted.

'Right away. Give me a moment.' Raman murmured.

'Alka ji or Kamal ji, who would go for the test, please?' Rajiv asked.

'I would go. Kamal ji is a diabetic, and he keeps pricking his fingers to check the diabetic levels in his blood. Let me cover for him, this one time.' Alka confirmed.

'Constable, take madam for a DNA test. Get her back here once it gets done.' Rajiv ordered.

While they were waiting, Raman gave the news that both Ravi and Saurav were traveling to Ranchi over the next couple of days, to be with the family.

'They were crying on the phone also and they could not express themselves well enough. I guess, by this evening, they would confirm their plans. They might be at Ranchi the day after if all goes well. So, Rajiv ji, you might as well travel to Ranchi the day after.'

'I think that is a great idea. Kindly confirm their plans once you hear from them. It would be good to connect and get a perspective from flat mates. They were the closest, as you guys said, right?' Rajiv asked.

'Absolute bum-chums, if you can say so. They were guardians to one another. They were the best of friends, and both loved Radha as a staunch friend. Radha was always gaga about them and about their habits and mannerisms, good and bad. They liked one another's company and would spend their evenings together, come what may. Things had changed slightly after Radha got serious with Akshay, though.' Raman narrated with clear diction and a lot of warmth. He was hurting, and I knew it.

I told the families to move to take the body, once Alka ji was back, and I went out saying I had a lot of work to do. I drove out of the thana.

The two families took Radha's body to Ranchi that afternoon to perform her last rites in the best way possible. The family thought of performing the last rites the next day and Raman informed Ravi and Saurav of the same. They confirmed they would reach Raman's place the next morning. They wanted to be present for the last rites ceremony. The family informed me of the developments, and I also confirmed my presence for the last rites of Radha.

I felt enraged at whatever happened to Radha. Fact that I had no real leads till now was hurting me. Rather than get into another round of drinks in the evening, I thought it better to call up Diya and organize some evening plans. We met at around 7 pm at my place and the night was still young.

'Diya, it is an absolute delight to have you over. You know, through the day I have been thinking about you, while trying to solve a knotty case and handle the girl's parents. You have blown my mind and you know it!'

'Inspector, be careful what you say. You have a right to remain silent and whatever you say can be used against you.'

Diya bit her luscious and full lips, leaving a wonderful effect on me. I just could not stop myself from kissing her for over a few minutes, I guess. Both got exhausted just by that deep kiss.

I laid out the table and poured her some white citrus wine from the French vineyards. I poured myself also some wine. I usually like scotch, neat and without even ice. I like it warm and full. It was a different day. I do not believe in love, but this was something as well. I cannot say it is infatuation at my age, so I guess it is next only to love. It could be a deep connection or just an incarnation of physical requirement. I had never felt it in the past, and I enjoyed my time with Diya. She is an intelligent and a witty person. I think she has spent her educational years in one of the larger cities in India, or in the Western countries. She is not a Latehar candidate, and of that, I was sure. I, however, did not want to go beyond our time together. Getting to know one another will happen in due course. Once she was comfortable, she would get me a peek into her past and her present life. I will not ask her questions myself, and I must keep my detective hat away for a bit.

We got drunk together, while she sat in my lap and I kept hugging her tightly, while drinking and watching some dance contest. My hands would find her body often and she loved the gentle caressing and holding. She sat snugly on my lap, and we kissed many times. We held on our own for a couple of hours before we went to the bed, having had some dinner.

These were the best hours of my life, and I knew I had to make the most of it while it lasted. I felt inquisitive about her education and other stuff, as also her background. I also thought whether it was kind of honey trap for me. I was, however, not into any spying related job, so the honey trap was a thing of my wild imagination.

Diya was not interested in talking about my past or telling me about herself. She was taking it as it went, and my inquisitiveness had to be kept at bay. It only increased her hold over me. I learned to take it one night at a time.

CHAPTER 12

21 February 2010: 13:00 Hrs
This is time, the narrator, speaking.

The procession began from Raman's house to Harmu Road for the cremation. It took them under half an hour to reach there, from Raman's house at Ratu Road. Rajiv was there for the cremation, and he met Ravi and Saurav there. They were in an awful shape, and it seemed they had had their fair share of grief. After almost half an hour, while the cremation process was still on, Rajiv asked Ravi and Saurav out for a brief walk. Once they came out, he saw it was a high traffic zone and it would be difficult for them to talk, standing there. So, he got the two of them on his jeep and they went towards a small restaurant in Kishoreganj nearby. He knew it was not proper for them to have food after a cremation, but he said he only meant to have a chat for a moment. Thereafter, he would drop them at Raman's house.

'Bhaiya (brother), give us some chai. We would not have food as of now, but we need a quiet table in a corner where even your waiters would not trouble us.

Are you clear? This is police business. Hope I do not have to remind you!' Rajiv thundered at the counter clerk, who was the owner of the restaurant; and walked towards an empty table that had exactly three seats. The hotel owner scurried to get tea for the three of them and he kept himself away from the counter thereafter.

'Ravi and Saurav, how well did you know Radha? Well, do not answer that question. I am aware you guys were flat mates. It has a different connotation in these backward places, but you guys are in a westernized society, so it is different for you guys there. I am not judging you guys or even Radha here. I know it is all a mentality and some people have it while others are modern, and they have an open outlook. It is your life, and no one has a right to say anything to you guys. Also, you are all adults, so no preaching here.

I just need to know when it was last that you guys spoke to her. Did you speak to her when she was here at Ranchi or while she was at Netarhat? How did she sound like and did either of you feel anything amiss in her voice? Was she happy with Akshay or was she pretending to like him because, Saurav was not yet ready to embrace her? I need the truth and fast!'

'You are correct when you say that I loved her, and I had professed my love for her a day later than the day Akshay asked her. I had lost that game and I was aware of the consequences. I was sad about not being able to have her in my life, but I was okay with it, as it was because of my own decisions. It was all because of the actions I had taken and the paths that I had chosen. She was not wrong, and she had every right to live her life the way she wanted to lead and with the guy she wanted to be with. She, like everyone else, had absolute freedom with her choices. Your choices make the man you become–as they say. She was a strong and an independent lady and she was a cynosure of my eyes. However, I was clear in my head that she would remain my best friend and my first but unrequited love. Saying that is also not fully appropriate, though, as she waited for me to take a call, and for quite a while. So, that charm worked either way, but Akshay eventually blew her away. Akshay was good, and while I was not happy seeing him in a position that I dreamed of being in, he had her in his arms as an arm candy. Only that she could never just be an arm candy. She was beauty and brains together. She was better than Akshay, or so I always felt.

Akshay had his own personality, and he was good. Ravi also liked him and the four of us were okay with one another. Akshay had begun his date routines often, and slowly both of us felt lonely at our PG. We slowly learned to cope with her being away from us. She would marry and stay at a different house. They had already started identifying their appropriate location for home. Somewhere from where either of their offices were equidistant. So, we were preparing to lose her to Akshay. Our life was going to change for the worse while her life was possibly going to change for the better, or so we thought.

However, whatever has happened beats us and we are so sorry to see her in this state. It is beyond comprehension, and it is unacceptable. We are there for any help, as you please. We also want to see the culprits behind bars. All of them. All the villagers, whoever has committed this ghastly and dastardly crime. They have given unimaginable pain and the worst couple of hours of life to that great soul. They could not live a decent life. If they have done this to please Gods, I know Gods are not there with them,' saying thus, Saurav started sobbing. His eyes were red, and he had tears in his eyes.

Rajiv gave him a hard look and then turned to Ravi.

'Inspector Rajiv, we could not sleep ever since we heard about this heinous crime. What have reduced ourselves to in this twenty-first century? Humans are going to the dogs! Well, to answer your question, I had spoken to Radha while she was still in Ranchi. She told me about her plans to visit Netarhat over the next couple of days, while also telling me her family members wanted them to go there with them; but she was happy she refused. She wanted to go there with Akshay and with no one else. She wanted to see the sunrise point in Akshay's arms, and she wanted to feel the Netarhat air and its pristine falls and jungles only with Akshay. This would have been their way of pre-marriage memories. She had it all sorted. I feel Akshay was just going through the motions, as he would not have been the decision maker. Radha was a strong p-type.' Ravi mentioned.

'What is a p-type?' Inspector asked.

'Personality type.' Ravi mentioned.

'And you, Saurav?'

'Yes, I spoke to her a day later. She was getting her luggage ready. I remember, having tried to reason with her not to go alone, as there could be Maoists or some other dangers lurking in the woods. She did not listen to me. All she said was a lot of tourists went there often and the place was very good. She had decided and no one could have dissuaded her.' Saurav surmised.

'Were you guys planning to come to Ranchi by any chance, while she was there?' Inspector asked.

'We were thinking about surprising her, but she did not allow us enough time to do that. She left us before we could get here. This is a devastating turn of events. Do you know where Akshay is? Uncle Raman told me he is missing since that same evening. No one seems to have seen him at Netarhat or anywhere else. His parents are increasingly worried, and they are going back to Mumbai tomorrow. They told us they have received no ransom calls till now. They also fear the worst but pray for the best.' Ravi blurted out.

'So, were the two of you there at Bangalore together while she was here at Ranchi or Netarhat?' Inspector asked.

'No, Saurav had gone out for a couple of days on a trip to find a job. He is in search of a job in the financial industry. I was there at the PG. Mr. Murali would vouch for it.' Ravi mentioned with prying eyes, looking towards Saurav.

'Yes, I had gone to Mumbai to meet some consultants to help me with my job search. I had a couple of meetings lined up.' Saurav said.

'Okay, so get me to speak to those people whom you met while you were there in Mumbai, Saurav. And Ravi, who is this Mr. Murali?' Inspector asked.

'Mr. Murali is our caretaker in the PG. He is also an excellent cook.' Ravi mentioned.

'Inspector Rajiv, I am sorry, but I cannot get you to speak to any consultant. I had my meetings lined up there, but they got caught up in other business and they could not meet me. I spoke to them over the phone, and they assured me they would get me a job. That's about it. I went back to Bangalore thereafter and was with Ravi.' Saurav mentioned.

'Interesting! So, you were in Mumbai while Radha was in Netarhat. Also, you do not have any witnesses. Share your flight ticket with me, along with a copy of the boarding pass for both sides of travel. That would be all. I would now drop you to Raman's house.' Inspector mentioned.

'But Inspector sahib, I cannot share my boarding pass. I have not kept it to myself. I would have thrown it at an airport dustbin for all I care. Am I in trouble here, Inspector?' Saurav asked.

'You are not in trouble, Saurav or Ravi, as you guys were her guardian angels. You can never be in trouble. I wish to close the Bangalore chapter, so all this evidence makes sense from that angle. Just share your flight ticket with me. I would take care of the rest. C'mon, let us leave now.'

They walked towards the parked jeep. Rajiv kept fifty bucks note at the counter and left.

Rajiv had to travel back to Latehar the same evening, and he had come prepared. Once bitten, twice shy. He could take an army of Maoists that evening with his massive preparation. Rajiv went to Raman's house with Ravi and Saurav. He stayed there for a while, interacting with the people who had assembled by then. Rajiv had changed into white kurta and pajama, fit for the occasion. He looked downright handsome, young, and in shape. He saw some young women drooling over him, while they should have cried hoarsely, hurting their throat and eyes. India was changing by the day and girls were powerful.

CHAPTER 13

22 February 2010: 13:00 Hrs
This time again it is time, the narrator, speaking.

Saurav had sent his flight tickets to Rajiv. Ravi and Saurav spent some time with Akshay's family while they were there till a day earlier. They stayed back at Ranchi for a couple of days to console the grieving parents. They were hurting themselves as a very important part of their lives had been snatched away from them. It was difficult for Saurav and for Ravi as well. They had a chemistry amongst the three of them and they were going to miss Radha for life.

Ravi had become slightly protective of Saurav ever since the last interaction with Inspector Rajiv. He wanted to protect his best living friend from hell that Rajiv could give anyone, even remotely, related to Radha in her hour of death. Such was the power of a police inspector in a thana that he could do a lot of things and destroy people and their careers. Ravi had taken a hard look at Rajiv, and he figured he was an honest and dutiful officer. For the sake of fun, or for the sake of finding a culprit, Rajiv would do nothing.

He was a detective, and he would employ reason to go after anyone.

'Saurav, hope you are good. Look, I do not need to tell you this, but I would still say it. I regard you as my best buddy and your well-being is precious to me. We have just now seen how difficult it could be for either of us if we remove one of our own from our lives. We need to pick ourselves up and help Radha's parents to recover. Their world has shattered and while we are hurting, we cannot imagine what they are going through right now. Also, I just hope this Inspector gets off our back. Mate, it would have been great if you had kept your boarding pass. I think an inspector can always get it from your airlines now that he has your tickets. Let us not worry about it. Should I book the return tickets for tomorrow? What do you say?'

'Um, so I agree with you entirely. We need to help her parents recover while we are here. I think we can go back tomorrow. Slowly, Raman uncle and auntie also need to get out of all of this, but the more they see us; I guess the more they would feel bad. It would take its obvious toll on our lives as we knew it. Let's just book our tickets and move out.' Saurav agreed.

The house had several guests from outside the city and people from the neighborhood and others who knew the family. A lot of her schoolmates were there, and the house was always full of people. The family was grieving, and every visitor was grieving, too. The case was on the media, tirelessly for many days, on a loop, and Inspector Rajiv's life was not getting easy. Media was breathing down every step he took or every direction his jeep went. The local channels had tasked their teams at Latehar and at Netarhat. While they were covering the incident, media men had a party of their life, at the picturesque hill-station.

CHAPTER 14

12 April 2009: 17:00 Hrs (9 months back)

'Akshay, let me take you somewhere special. You have taken me to expensive restaurants, bars, and discos. I wish to take you someplace else today. I have been going there often, over the last couple of years and I feel happy spending some time there.' Radha mysteriously said.

Akshay felt mesmerized, looking at her full lips and beautiful skin. He knew she was a powerful personality, but he was slowly getting to know her better. He was trying to look through her imposed image of a strong p-type and of a go-getter. Akshay was aware she billed 2000 television sets to Shetty ji during her year-end billings. Her branch manager and her entire branch of Pukar TV had gone gaga over the go-to girl. She was riding the zenith of success early in her career. Akshay wanted to take a deeper look at the person Radha was. He could see streaks of childish behavior and exuberance. He had seen in her a genuine affection for her friends, and he knew she expected a lot from him.

Akshay wanted to know her better. He wanted to know her vulnerabilities and her evolution from a child. Was she always like what she was now? He wanted to know how she would react to bad times, to sudden misery or to death of a dear one. He wanted to know how much she could love her partner.

Radha wore an Indian dress that evening. It surprised Akshay, as he wanted to take her out for a movie and dining. They could even have gone to a pub.

Akshay was in love. He wished to give her the best things that life could provide, so he wanted to earn a lot and keep her in luxury. He knew she was different, but he wanted to match up and do well for both.

Radha took him to a temple nearby. They sat there in its prayer area for an hour in deep thoughts.

Radha was happy when she came out. She guided Akshay to a nearby golgappa (a famous savory) stall. She felt contented to have had golgappas while Akshay looked on. He would have golgappas at a premium restaurant, not by a roadside stall. This stall was using water from a bucket, and Akshay was not sure.

Radha then moved to an ice-cream stall and took an orange ice-cream. It was her favorite childhood ice-cream and while the world had moved to various types of chocolate and other ice-creams and natural creams, Radha still loved her childhood ice-cream.

Having had her ice-cream, Radha moved towards a small shop where the shop owner was cooking banana chips. She bought a small packet of banana chips and then told Akshay to take her to a nearby park. Radha wanted to take it easy that evening. She did not want to be chasing anything. She wanted to feel nature, and she wanted to exult in its vicissitudes.

Weather was decent, and it was around dusk. They initially sat on a side bench in the park and took the view in. Akshay watched Radha longingly. He saw in her glowing face a person who was honest and fond of a basic life. He knew while she was chasing her sales targets; she believed in simple things in life, and she was not so luxury oriented. While Radha was in the park, she was just holding Akshay's hand and looking towards the setting sun. She wanted to take it all in that evening. Her decision to slow down, if only just for a day, had worked like a charm for her. She felt good and charged up for an eventful night.

It was 8 pm, and they went to a dhaba (small roadside restaurant) that sometimes the three musketeers used to go to. Radha told Akshay to accompany him, just to see her life, if only for a day. She loved her life the way it was, and she was in no mood to allow it to be completely taken over by a different life. She wished to continue to have a minimalistic life, that had room for both to enjoy some me-time and not keep running all their lives, for nothing.

While they had a masala tea, before dinner, Radha told Akshay a short story. 'Akshay, please listen to this story. There was a fisherman in a village by the sea. One morning, while he was fishing, another man came near him. The other person was well-dressed. He asked the fisherman why he did not go to a city nearby. The fisherman replied, asking how it would have helped him. The well-dressed person told him he could earn a lot more in a city. That would give him a better life. His earnings would grow overtime and he would become a rich man. The fisherman enquired what would he achieve if he were to become rich. The well-dressed person replied that once the fisherman was rich, he could relax and enjoy his life by the sea, fishing. The fisherman laughed heartily, saying he was already enjoying his time in the village, with no complications of a city life and he was already fishing.'

Radha looked at Akshay deeply. She wanted to hear his thoughts while the dhaba cook was cooking up a storm in there, challenging their olfactory nerves and doing justice to their hunger pangs.

Akshay was silent through the evening. He allowed Radha to show him the Radha way of life, which he knew, by then, differed from his own way of understanding her and that she was slowly showing him her true self. He was happy about it, and he wished to take his relationship to the next level. He thought he should propose soon. Would it be good there in the dhaba itself? Well, she loved the place, did she not?

While he was chewing over the thought, the waiter brought the kebabs and served them. They were hungry, so they just dug in. It was a lovely evening.

Akshay dropped Radha at her PG at 10 pm. He went in to just say "hi" to her best friends. He left soon after. Guys in the house were happy to see her back, and they knew she was early, so they took out a ludo from somewhere and had a gala night, shouting and laughing at one another.

CHAPTER 15

18 April 2009: 11:00 Hrs

'People, what is our plan for this weekend? Any ideas, or are we just lying at home, eating Mr. Murali's food and watching TV? I for one do not want to watch TV. As it is during my workdays, I watch a lot during my demonstrations to the in-store demonstrators, as a training for them or even to customers.' Radha mentioned, looking towards her buddies, Saurav and Ravi.

'Radha, I am surprised you have time for us this weekend. Is Akshay traveling?' Ravi smirked.

'Do not be so harsh on her. She is just trying to keep us happy whilst giving time to create a longer-term bond with Akshay. We must cut her some slack here.' Saurav retorted.

'Whose side are you on, Saurav? As it is, the last few weeks we have been in the house, doing exactly what Radha is saying today.' Ravi was quick in his reaction.

'Guys, take it easy. I do not have any plans for today and I wanted to know whether we want to go out for a meal or relax here and take it easy.' Radha mentioned. She was in her tees and short pants. It was her normal daily clothing that she loved for its comfort. Her face glowed that morning and she looked resplendent. Her skin looked baby soft, and her face had a magical feel. She looked ethereal. She must have had a good nap over the last night, or so, Saurav felt. Or was it Akshay who was having a salubrious effect on her? He knew he had lost her, as she never looked so ethereal, calm, and composed. It was love and one knew it does wonders for one's overall look and personality. Radha had changed for the better. She had reduced her pungent nature and had become relaxed and loving. She had become caring and mature; her persona clearly reflected she was in love, and Saurav had lost his chance, for real.

The bell rang that same moment while Saurav was still thinking about Radha, and not about her just asked question. Ravi was wondering what had happened to both Radha and Saurav.

Ravi opened the door.

'Hi Akshay, come on in. You are most welcome to help us create our plan for the day. Any plan that you make having us together or taking Radha out would mean creating our plan by default, you see!' Ravi almost scorned at Akshay.

Akshay waited a second longer at the door before getting in, but then he saw Radha and just walked in. He ignored the comment from Ravi and walked up to Radha. She was standing next to a dining chair. He took her right hand and guided her towards a cozy corner in the living area. While she stood there looking all dazed and perplexed at what had just happened, Akshay went down his knees.

Saurav and Ravi took out their mobile cameras. One of them started clicking pictures while the other put it on video mode. It was an important day and a very meaningful event for Radha, and they thought they could do at least as much.

Radha was now in a trance with mouth agape. She just looked at Akshay, who looked all romantic, and he had taken out a diamond ring by then.

'I cannot sit in this awkward position all day, sweetheart. Would you accept to marry me, my princess? I await thy order and I would keep your honor in your decision, either way. So, please do not worry. Let me know whether you accept to marry me, for life. I wish to betroth you and I speak to thee in ever so gentle voice. Would you grant my wish, my queen?' Akshay made a mockery of himself, did a bit of caricature, and won his princess who said she accepted to get engaged for her life.

Akshay inserted the ring in her ring finger, and it fitted her like a charm. She was amazed and dumbfounded.

The two guys clapped and shouted while Mr. Murali also came and blessed the couple.

'Akshay, when did you take the size for her ring? It fit her like a charm. You are a smart guy! I have to give that to you.' Ravi blurted out.

'Yes Akshay, you never took the size of my finger, but this one is just like made for me. How did you do it, or was it providential? God-ordained?' Radha was overjoyed, and she did not want to keep her thoughts to herself. She joined in the banter with Ravi.

'Guys, cut me some slack here. I have obviously held her hands till now, but we have not gone beyond that. In such great evenings on a bench in a park or in a movie theater in its dim lights, we have not as much as kissed each other. But point granted there that I have held her hand and I think I got lucky with the size.' Akshay took in all the praise with equanimity and kept up with the charming visage.

'May I invite the three of you today for a lunch? I wish to take you guys out as you are family, like guardians, you see?' Akshay asked while having a salubrious charm that worked wonders on Radha.

'I think you guys should carry on. We do not wish to get between you people. It is a very important day in your lives, and you should totally enjoy. Do not carry us with you guys today as luggage.' Ravi mentioned rather impetuously.

'Ravi, stop! Akshay has requested both of you to be a part of our celebrations. Celebrations do not work without family. I do not need to stress here that you guys are my family. So, cut the crap and get ready. Akshay, excuse me for some time. I would change and come. Please watch TV or have some tea. Mr. Murali, could you please serve some tea or coffee to Akshay? I would get back really quick.'

'Radha, I have prepared some *kokum* (a fruit-based beverage) as it is such a nice day for you and for Akshay. Please have some. I am giving it to all of you within a minute.' Mr. Murali spoke. Radha thanked Mr.

Murali and went to change. Saurav and Ravi also went to change into their better clothes.

Saurav sat in the living area and spoke to his parents, informing them Radha's acceptance. They wanted to speak to her, but he said he needed a bit of time as they were going out with her friends. He promised he would get them to speak to Radha during the day.

He had his kokum, and he thanked Mr. Murali profusely. By then, Ravi and Saurav had come. They sat around Akshay and had a discussion going while Radha took her time. She came out after almost half an hour, dressed in a light pink-colored lehenga (Indian ankle-length skirt like dress). She looked stunning. Akshay got up, looking at her, and went up to give her a peck on her cheeks.

'By Joe, someone has collared up this afternoon, well, without the collar! I meant, dressed up and why should you not, Radha? It makes sense. So, what do you want us to do today? We would be like your brothers or like your friends?' Ravi enquired, just so that he was clear.

'I do not want to represent her as her brother, but you can, Ravi. It is up to you. I am happy being her friend and flatmate.' Saurav interrupted.

'You guys are my best buddies, and you would stay that way. I am not looking for a brother in you people. Having my brother here right now and my parents would have been so good. How I miss them today!'

'We would go to Ranchi and meet all of them. But for now, let us all go out and enjoy.'

CHAPTER 16

27 February 2010: 13:00 Hrs (Present day)

I knocked. The house help opened the door. I asked him about Saurav and before he could answer, or react, I barged in with my team of officers from Bengaluru Police. Ravi and Saurav had just completed their lunch and were still on the dining table.

I had a search warrant. Before Ravi or Saurav could react, my team searched the entire house. I found nothing that was of value to the Police. Ravi had couriered all of Radha's clothes and all her stuff to Ranchi via a local courier.

They did not find any incriminating evidence in Saurav's or Ravi's room as well. The policemen went outside while Rajiv was in the living room. Ravi and Saurav were sitting in front of him like babies in front of their new teacher.

'Saurav, I can take you into custody immediately.'

'What did I do, inspector?'

'You tell me? Why did you lie to me?'

'When did I lie to you, Inspector Rajiv? I even sent you my tickets.'

'Now, there, it shows on you. You are a first time criminal, and you do not have an idea how things work, right?'

'I do not understand what you are accusing me of.'

'I would come to that. Now, tell me why you did not travel to Mumbai?'

'I went there but as luck would have it, I did not get to meet anyone else. I might not have got into this trouble.'

'We checked with the airlines. These tickets never got used. No one went on these tickets and the airlines forfeited the money on account of no-show. I understand you are unemployed as of now and you still wasted almost ten grand. Why?'

'Oh, yes, you are correct. I did not travel to Mumbai. I was here in Bangalore itself, at my friend's place. However, as I had told Radha and Ravi I was going to Mumbai, so I had to continue with my lie, even if it meant losing that money.'

'No, you did not have to, Saurav! Why would you waste your money and put yourself in trouble, because you had mentioned to us you were going to Mumbai?' Ravi interjected.

There came a tight slap across Saurav's face. I was livid, and I could not take Saurav's lies any more.

'Wait, Inspector, let him tell the truth.' Ravi was trembling by then.

'Rajiv, I am not lying.' Saurav mentioned.

He got another slap instantaneously. By then, his nose started bleeding. Saurav felt pain, and he dug in his head in his palm and started crying.

'We have your phone details, Saurav. You were in Ranchi and then in Netarhat. Why did you kill your best buddy and her fiancé? Is it a love-triangle here?' Rajiv thundered.

'It was a love-triangle of his own making, Inspector. Radha liked him and he liked Radha, but he never accepted that. He kept her waiting. Finally, she moved on and Akshay just had called her after many years, just then.' Ravi mentioned.

'I did not kill Radha. It was a love triangle of my making, and I was at fault. Things moved quickly after Akshay came into her life. By the time I told Radha about my love for her, she had started to like Akshay. I mentioned my love to her, eventually, in front of Ravi, but that was way too late. We agreed to remain friends and nothing else.'

'Why did you travel to Ranchi, Akshay?' Rajiv asked.

'I went there to meet her parents and to have a chat with her. I wanted to impress upon them to agree to marrying their daughter with me and not with Akshay. I was a fellow Ranchi'ite, you see. She had a soft corner for me, and I thought I could move her decision into accepting me. I was wrong in my assumptions, I guess. While I reached her Ranchi house, I saw from outside a happy family, what with Akshay, Radha, her brother, sister-in-law, and parents all enjoying their time together. Akshay had already made his way into their hearts, and they looked happy that Radha had found him. Radha also had a great chemistry with him, and I think it happened so quickly because they were from the same college. When I saw all this, I thought it was a mistake and I should not have even attempted this. I did not meet Radha or her family. I went back to my house.' Saurav mentioned.

'Why did you go to Netarhat in that case, Saurav? If you could not meet her at Ranchi, why would you still follow her to Netarhat? You wanted a revenge, is it not the case, Saurav?' Inspector asked.

'Hell, no! I was at Ranchi, and I knew of her plans for Netarhat. I spoke to my parents, and we all went to Netarhat for just one evening. I wanted to go there, and my parents agreed. Check with them if you wish to. They do not know about my mindset about Radha or even that I had gone there to meet her. They only know that I was feeling down because of joblessness, and I went there to meet them and relax.'

'I can take you into custody. The case looks clean. You were a deranged lover who could not see her happy with someone else, hence the crime. What I do not understand is why you did what you did to her. If you had to kill both, you could have taken an easy option for them, like putting bullets in them. Why did you kill her after giving her hell and where on earth has Akshay disappeared? Are you still hiding him? Where is he? Come on, now it is time to confess. Tell us everything.' I motioned towards him my phone, putting it on recording mode.

'I do not know why you are trying to get a confession from me here. I understand from your background that you are one of the few thinking detectives in the department. Why would you take a short-cut here?' Saurav asked, and he looked genuine.

'You are better than many criminals, as you can use your expressions to hide what you are. You do an admirable work or hiding the truth. All these are lies, we know. Come to the point and let us know what happened that eventful evening. Did you call them somewhere, or you just spotted them and carried them somehow therefrom?' Inspector asked.

'Inspector, again I am telling you, you are mistaken. Arrest me if you must, but I would get out on bail tomorrow morning. You have nothing on me, apart from my own foolish lie. Once and for all, let me tell you the truth. I did not meet Radha or Akshay my entire trip to Ranchi and Netarhat. I saw them at Ranchi, but I did not meet them. I am not your killer here and he is roaming free somewhere. This case has become intricate, and I understand your position. Now, if you would excuse me, I would go to my room for a siesta. Mr. Murali can cook some lunch for you and your other friends while I take a quick nap. Would it be okay?' Saurav asked.

I somehow felt Saurav was telling me the truth. I told Saurav not to leave the city. I also asked him to go to a local police station every few days and mark an attendance.

Ravi looked differently at Saurav, and both went to their rooms.

CHAPTER 17

18 APRIL 2009: 21:30 Hrs (10 months back)

'Guys, I need to head back to the PG. It has been a crazy day. Loved every bit. Thanks, Akshay, for taking us out as a family. I have a long day tomorrow as well, so I would give it a pass now. You guys carry on and go ahead with your movie plans. I need some rest.' Ravi mentioned.

'I am coming with you, Ravi. Let the love birds cuckoo this evening. We have had our bit of fun for today. While I cannot say I have a long day tomorrow, but that reminds me to go back to that firm's office to meet the regional head. I am a bit surprised why he has not sent out my appointment letter yet.' Saurav mentioned rather glumly.

'Do not worry, Saurav. I hope he hands over the letter tomorrow itself. I could also kind of come back to the PG with you guys. We all had a hectic day. What do you say, Akshay?' Radha asked.

'Sweetheart, relax. We would watch a short movie, a good Hollywood flick. So, do not worry. I would drop you home. Also, I would have loved if you guys could have accompanied us.' Akshay added.

'Guys, no sweat! We have had a day and we want to relax a bit. Allow us to get back and please drop Radha after the movie. And Radha, no hanky-panky, please. You know we are your guardians and today we have worked that part well.' Ravi mentioned, laughing out loud. They all had a hearty laugh and Akshay and Radha moved towards the theater while Saurav and Ravi went towards the PG.

'Hey, you need to give me some space to keep my arm on this arm-rest. Do not assume it is yours only.' Akshay winked at Radha, and she caught his eye movements in the dim lights. She allowed him to keep his arm on the armrest and cozied into him a little. A bit later, Akshay took her hand in his and fondled with her fingers. Then he caressed her upper leg with ever so gentle movements. Radha was quiet, and she had an urge to feel Akshay's body. She kept still and silent, trying to watch the movie. Akshay saw he was not being stopped, so he felt her side body through his right arm. She did not stop him and snuggled up to him. In a sudden movement, Akshay brought his lips close to hers, while watching other people who were at a vantage point and who could look at him. Radha could feel his breath under hers and she realized what Akshay was about to do. She also looked around a bit and then gave Akshay a sudden kiss on the lips. It was a hurried kiss, and it did not last for Akshay to feel her enough. He felt it did not carry his feeling through and he understood why she did what she did.

It was her way of saying that they still had time to get into a proper and thorough kissing. She was okay only with a bit of public display of affection. She was not prepared to go with the whole hog. Radha was someone who took it slowly, and she wanted to be certain of her steps and her priorities in life. She wanted to control the proceedings as per her pace, and she did not want to be led into something she did not like yet.

Akshay straightened up while Radha continued to hold on to him. She knew much lesson was okay for Akshay for the day and she was only trying to let him know his limits. She also wanted him not to be upset, and she knew she could keep him happy. Her mother used to tell her, as an adult, the life of a girl asks for various sacrifices. A girl sacrifices many times in her lifetime, to allow her family life to be protected and her folks loved and well-fed. Her mother's teachings had kept her in good stead in her various relationships, and she had never allowed herself to be carried away. She wanted a secure relationship with all its goodness. She did not want any rash decision or impulse to take her life away in a flash. Akshay's training was a part of her mother's teachings and Radha had matured into a woman.

Radha was confident and comfortable in her relationships, and she knew how much those relationships would be worth and how many sacrifices they would ask.

Akshay later left Radha at her PG and showed he was a truly nice guy. He, for once, did not flinch, and he kept his chin up. He knew he could not allow any rash decisions to turn into guilt in the future. Akshay was protective of his relationship with Radha. He knew he had found a life partner in her and he would do nothing to harm that equation.

CHAPTER 18

04 March 2010: 11:30 Hrs (Present day)

'Sir, we have been keeping a tab on the phone calls of all the family members of Radha and Akshay. It was as per your approval. We have found something interesting. They are getting phone calls from various sim-cards and then they do not use those sim-cards for any other calls. Either Akshay himself is talking to his parents or the abductors are. How else can we explain such phone calls on an almost organized basis, twice a day, at 10 am and at 6 pm?' One of my constables reported to me.

'That looks interesting. Do they talk? As we tap their phone, we must record their conversation, right? Wait, I understand, so these calls are possibly only reminder calls and then his parents use their phone or some other phone to call that number. Therefore, we do not get to hear in. Now, that is quite smart for his parents. It must be Akshay or his abductors. Let us speak to his parents now. Get his father on call with me. 'Kamal ji, I have an interesting observation to make. Congratulations on finding your son. Thank God he is alive. Why is he still hiding? Why does he not get there and meet you guys yet? What is holding him back?' Rajiv asked politely.

'What are you even saying, Rajiv ji? I am surprised. Is it a question to me or you are answering yourself over something that I have no clue about? Let us not play hide and seek here. I know you have called with some intent. Let us talk about it without beating about the bushes.' Kamal answered.

'I like your style, Kamal ji. Let me come to the point. Why are you hiding these phone calls from us? What is cooking?'

'So, you know, we have been getting these random phone calls and then we cannot get in touch with those phone numbers. It always says that the number is not in use. We felt frustrated. We earlier thought it was Akshay or his abductors calling us. Both of us hoped they would give us some signal that we can use to respond to them effectively. I have kept money ready, only that I could not speak to them. Reema is now in poor health, unable to cope up with this long absence of Akshay. I am ill as well, but I keep comforting her, saying all would be well. Tell me how to figure it out. If it is Akshay and if he is trying to get in touch with us through these random calls, I do not know how to get back in touch with him. Also, if it is their abductors, they are from a different world, as I cannot decipher their signals. So, I implore upon you as the chief investigator of this murder case to help us with our predicament. We want to get a closure. We want our son back. Help us get there, please!' Kamal started sobbing on the phone.

'We would find him, Kamal ji, and I hope, alive and well. Had it been a murder, we would have found his body by now. Had it been an abduction, we would have found his abductors by now. I do not have a single open case against my name, and I assure you I would find Akshay even if he is hiding in the earth's underbelly. My only issue is, now I have a feeling there might be an involvement of Akshay in this crime. He might not be alone, but he could be involved.' Rajiv said.

'Please do not say such things. As it is, we are ill, and all of this is not helping us. God help Akshay. I hope he is good, and it does not involve him in the heinous crime. He is our son, and he is someone of very high morals. He would never engage in something as bad as this. We are sure he is paying a heavy price for no reason. The sooner he comes back, the better it would be. It would help you close the case.' Kamal mentioned.

I disconnected the phone and got thinking. I kept revising the connections of people in the case, multiple times over. Then I zoomed out of his office to my superior's office. I took his permission to speak to my counterpart in Mumbai. I arranged for two constables to monitor Kamal's flat in Andheri East.

I revealed little to my superior. I only said I had a hunch, and I wished to just do a basic follow up to get over it. If I am not mistaken, I think my boss is already in awe of my deductive skills, and he somehow knows what I called a hunch was a by-product of a careful assessment of the case. I spoke to Radha's parents as well. They did not get any suspicious calls. Neither were they aware of any such calls at Akshay's place. They were in deep distress, and they were not keeping well.

News channels and newspapers had carried out their versions of the developing story and all quoted me in their own way. I dislike these journalists who keep giving any script their own spin, and then they become the judge, jury and executioner themselves. I do not enjoy being on the other end of such publicity. As it is, I feel I have taken too long already to crack the case open. I have traveled to Netarhat thrice within such few days and I have gone deep in the woods on various hunches as I now like to call it. However, it produced little result.

My other hunch of Saurav did not work. I would have liked it, but Saurav was punctual with his attendance at the police station at Bangalore.

I need a breakthrough, and I feel it is near, yet far. I deserve a victory for all the hard work I have put in this case. I also know this case needs more time and more attention and I will not get thorough without solid homework. I have never shied away from work, but I have still not found a fissure in the story. Finding Akshay is of prime importance now and I must do something about it. I feel there could be some answers in Mumbai and that I either need to bug Kamal's home or the constables there would do their duty and report back soon.

CHAPTER 19

05 March 2010: 19:30 Hrs

'Sir, we saw the family going out of house twice today. Once around 10 o'clock in the morning and next at 6 pm. They went out like a normal morning and evening walk in their joggers. They looked harried though, and we saw them going into a telephone booth after ten minutes both the times.' Constable from Mumbai spoke to Rajiv.

'Okay, that is great. Just speak to the telephone booth owner and get the telephone number that was called by Kamal ji. Send me a message with those numbers. I would be waiting. I need it right away.' I ordered.

I got two different numbers from Mumbai. I asked my men to check the numbers and to let me know the details that they could figure out. I got a call soon enough saying that both the sim-cards were not in use. The only thing common was that the same numbers had given them a few rings, and they had disconnected. Thereafter, these numbers received only one call each from a telephone booth in Mumbai.

I was confident there was more to the story, and that I should go to Mumbai soon. I did not want to speak to Kamal or Reema. I wanted to meet them directly at their residence or to catch them in their act and then lead the interrogation from there. Somehow my sixth sense or my deductive process was enough to get him to plan a Mumbai visit soon. I knew the story would get legs in Mumbai.

I spoke to my boss and took his approval to travel. I spoke to my counterpart in Mumbai Police thana in Kamal's area of residence. It was all sorted, and I looked forward to the travel.

As an after-thought, I asked my team to tap the phones of both Saurav and Ravi. I wanted to keep myself informed if there was anything that I needed to know. I did not like surprises, and it would be good to be aware.

CHAPTER 20

22 July 2009: 19:30 Hrs (8 months back)
'You are welcome to my small house, Radha. Let me just tidy it up a bit while you can relax here. Can I fetch you a glass of water? I did not go out today as I was not feeling well. It is great that you came by.' Akshay was excited and he spluttered.

'Akshay, relax. You do not have to tidy it up or to get me water or anything. Just sit over here. I need to know how tidy you are normally at your place. I am surprised that I did not find your clothes and shoes all over the living and dining room. Let me check out your bedroom and your washroom,' saying thus Radha just barged into his bedroom. She saw multiple posters of his favorite movie stars. He had Rambo posters all over the place. So, she knew Sylvester Stallone was his favorite actor. She knew he liked action movies, as he had always taken her to action movies.

She also saw a couple of Marilyn Monroe posters along with Madhuri Dixit's. Radha had a clear idea of the man that Akshay was. It impressed her to see that on a Sunday evening, his bed was neat. It impressed her to see his study area. He had a stack of books, fiction and non-fiction, and he had a table lamp. It meant he was a regular user of the table and it showed why he used to stand straight, as he was in a habit of sitting straight and reading. She was quite the opposite, as she enjoyed lounging on sofas or on her bed and reading stuff. Chair and table with a lamp were not her thing.

Akshay was staring at her all this while. She moved to see his attached bathroom, and she felt the steam from a possible hot-water bath. The aroma was overpowering, and she felt taken.

Akshay realized she liked what she felt, and he held her tightly in his arms. She gave herself in to the pleasure of two young people held together by a deep bond between them. Her body longed for his lean, but in-shape body. He was strong, and she felt she was in an erotic location, trying to pull herself away from such emotions. A part of her brain said, let me get back to safety. The other part of her heart said she liked the guy, and they were young people with needs. She could give in to the pleasures.

Akshay felt her body and his hands were moving all over her. He fondled with her breasts and then moved his lips towards her belly button. He sucked it in hard and then moved his lips in a passionate display of pulsating energy. It churned her stomach and Radha started groaning softly. He could feel her breath over him. His lips and his hands were doing the talking as he pushed her against a wall and felt her skin. His legs were moving now, touching her legs, caressing her intermittently, feeling the pleasures of a soft and beautiful body. He had kept his lips away from hers and he moved her body to face her back. His lips felt her nape softly. She let out a soft groan while his fingers moved towards her back and he put his hands inside her jeans.

Radha stopped him right there and went running out to the living area. She was perspiring, and she did not want to give in to his charms soon. She believed in the institution of marriage, and she knew she was pushing Akshay to the limits. Akshay walked in only after washing his face and picking up a diet cola from the refrigerator.

'What would you have for dinner, Radha? Can we like, talk? Look, I am sorry if I went beyond my limits there. Also, do not beat yourself on what just happened. We are young and fond of each other. These things happen to a lot of us at our age. I know you want us to know our limits and stay within them. We would stay within those defined limits. But can we at least have a kiss or two, when we really need one, or is that also beyond the middle-class decency? I am also from the middle-class, so please do not take an offence here!' Akshay looked like a kid asking for a little more love from his teacher, ever so honest and in need of what he wanted.

Radha gave in to his demand and kissed him passionately. They were tongue-tied for a long time, seeking each other, and wanting to forget everything around them. Radha could feel the urge to let go of her self-imposed restrictions, but she felt it was necessary. She knew they would travel soon to Ranchi and their parents would finalise their marriage. It was only a matter of time and she wanted to take her time and tread carefully.

Akshay ordered some pizza, and they had a nice time, cuddling and feeling each other, while watching the movie *Beta*, wherein Madhuri Dixit had an erotic dance number with her favorite co-star Anil Kapoor, going as '*Dhak dhak karne laga (heart goes kaboom!).*'

The song reminded them of their state, and they knew they had to wait for their marriage to happen. There was nothing that was going to take it away from them, and patience was a virtue. They would love it when they waited for it and then achieved it. Imagine how they would enjoy their honeymoon, Radha used to oft-repeat.

Akshay knew she was a good girl, and he had found in her, his soulmate. He had to take care of her emotions and of her attitudes and preferences with care. He knew boys might not understand a lot of such feelings that girls had, but he wanted to be on the right-side of her thoughts and of her opinion.

He dropped Radha to her PG. He did not feel like going inside. She gave him a peck on his cheeks and thanked him for a nice evening spent together.

Akshay sped back home, and he took out a videocassette of an X-rated movie. He watched it for about half an hour, voyeuristically enjoying it and thinking about the time he could have had with Radha that evening. Having got intimate and having felt her body made his mind go bananas. He could not contain his happiness at what happened to him, and he wished to revel in that state for a while. He slept late that night, choosing to go for a sleep at almost 1 am.

As luck would have it, he had already booked Radha's and his tickets to Ranchi, to meet her parents, and to seek their permission for their marriage. Radha knew too well that her parents would be over-joyed to see their future son-in-law and agree to a quick ring-exchange ceremony.

The thought gave sleepless nights to Radha as well. She wished she could give in to the love that Akshay was doling out to her, but she kept ignoring it, on some pretext or the other. She only wished she could contain the excitement of Akshay without making him feel uncomfortable or without offending him. Radha could see that he was trying and that he was a good person.

She wondered whether she was as smitten with love as anyone could be or Akshay was more smitten by her than she could imagine. Well, guys, as time, I can tell you, she was clearly over-thinking, analyzing and deducting whist Akshay was truly in love, smitten by her, to the core, unable to get past it, rather drowning and drooling in her love, every minute of the day.

CHAPTER 21

31 December 2009: 19:30 Hrs (Three months back)

'You are not serious, are you? Come on, babe! Today is 31st December, for God's sake. It is a special day, as an entire year of our lives is all but over. It was a good year as we reconnected, and we had such a lovely time throughout the year. Come on, Saurav and Ravi, she cannot be serious.' Akshay implored Radha to have non-vegetarian food. They were in the best possible pub in town, but it was also a Thursday and Radha did not eat non-vegetarian food on a Thursday. It was her prayer day, and she believed in it as her parents believed in it.

'We are not getting into that mess, Akshay. She likes her non-vegetarian food, and she loves this restaurant, but we have learned not to mess with her food choices. We give her the space she needs, which we believe you give her more than any of us. So, stop worrying about her and enjoy the evening. She cannot have a guilt here on having non-veg food because of you or, on the contrary, not having but kind of making sure that you spoil all our evening.' Ravi mentioned.

'I agree.' Saurav mentioned.

'I give in, and I am not unhappy about it, Radha. I only wanted you to enjoy the evening as much as us, but obviously not by making a tough choice. You know, food is delicious, and this prawn chilli is to die for. Tell me something, it is already 11 pm. Technically, after 12 am, the date changes. So, at 12:01 am, it would be a Friday. Would you have non-veg after that time? Does it work that way?' Akshay was curious.

'No, Akshay, it does not work that way. If we go by Hinduism, a day begins at dawn. So, this 12:01 am business does not work. Let us not worry about our food. I am thrilled to be spending this hour with my best friends and my fiancé and let us just go for the maximum fun. There is too much noise coming from inside. Let us finish our food and join the gang inside for some dance. We need to be on the floor to ring in the new year!' Radha said.

The team had their share of food and got on the dance floor. They had a blast while the world was having a great time. They were happy as Saurav had got a Senior Relationship Manager's role in Zebra Consulting Limited and he was enjoying his work. His High Net Worth Individual (HNWI) customers were happy as he had handled their portfolios well, even while he was out of a job. They were all appreciative of his work-ethics.

Ravi had an exceptional year, as his police contract had come through. So, while his private sector clients had dried up in a terrible year, the government contracts were alive and kicking. Ravi had got his internal promotion, and he just loved it.

Radha was a star performer in a dying company. She knew she had to jump ship, but she wanted to get married and only then, change over to a Korean company. The Indian TV companies were losing the day, and she knew the Koreans were doing brisk business. She loved her company and wanted to be with the firm for as long as she could have.

Akshay was having a great time with Radha, and he could not believe his luck. She was someone who was a dream come true for him and he knew they would soon travel to Ranchi, to seek approval from Radha's parents. They would tie the nuptial knot soon thereafter.

They had a great time, and they got back home at almost 3 am. It was a night to remember. The new year was their year, and they were going to make it work!

CHAPTER 22

8 MARCH 2010: 11:30 Hrs

'Sir, I had a good meeting with the local thana in-charge. I am going to meet Kamal ji and Reema ji, along with two constables from Mumbai Police. I will report to you if I have any findings and would travel back to Latehar only tomorrow evening.' I reported to my superior from Mumbai.

I waited outside Kamal's house for a moment, but barged in. I asked my constables to go around the flat in a jiffy, without giving them any time to figure out what hit them. I did not have a search warrant, and I did not want to wait for one.

The three of us zoomed into Kamal's apartment at 11.45 am and within 15 minutes, the two constables had gone out of the house. They were outside in the jeep, waiting for me to finish my discussion cum interrogation of Akshay's parents.

'Kamal ji, I apologize for my rude behavior earlier today. We did not have a search warrant, but we still had to figure out what was going on, and it is necessary to find your son, as he is our only clue to this case, dead or alive. We have to find him, and I do not give up easily.' I mentioned rather apologetically.

'That is ok. It just terrorized us, you see! We are not used to policemen suddenly barging into our house and we are under deep distress. In person, I wish to tell you something that I could not tell you earlier on the phone. See, I do not know how to handle this and therefore, I have to let you in on the predicament that I have.' Saying this, Kamal looked at Reema with a suspicious gaze.

Reema nodded, so Kamal continued. 'We have been getting some phone calls, almost continuously, every day twice. The calls are consistent, and they mostly come at around 10 am and at 6 pm. They come from a new number every day, rather every time. We know that you have tapped our phones, so we go out religiously, and call back the number. However, a full ring goes and then someone picks up the call. Thereafter, we keep saying hello and *beta* (son) and many other things. He listens to us for a full minute and then the phone goes dead silent. We cannot speak to anyone or contact anyone. I do not understand what is happening there. Is it Kamal himself, or is it his abductor? If it is Kamal, then we do not understand what he is afraid of. If it is one of his abductors, we do not understand why they do not ask for ransom and free my child?'

'Well, I have been thinking, and I came to only a couple of possibilities here. Before I narrate the possibilities, I must tell you we have found a DNA match on the shirt that was found soaked in blood. However, Akshay's DNA match was not there at the crime scene or anywhere near it. That only means Akshay was not there at the crime scene at the time of the crime. He might have been under detention somewhere else, and they beat him up.

That brings me to my two versions of the story as it unfolded then, and my recreation of the crime scene is not complete, but I know it is one of the two versions. According to the first version, maybe your son is alive and may be free as well, but they have specifically asked him not to speak to anyone. He checks in every day to just see that you people are okay, and you are managing your life without him. That comforts him, so he calls you twice every day. He is still not out of the grip of the killer, and they have warned him not to meet you or to meet anyone or even to speak to anyone. He knows the killer is dangerous, and he obeys him.

The other explanation is that he himself was amongst the killer troupe, and while he loves you guys and wishes to speak to you, he cannot, for fear of being caught. His life, as such, is over, but he still cannot distance himself from either of you.

There is no third explanation. It is not the abductor who calls you. It is your son who calls you. That gives us a direction in this case. Akshay is alive, and either dangerously involved in the killing or he is under the influence of the killer, terrorized of consequences, and he is in hiding. For all we know, he might have started a new life already by changing his documents and masking himself differently. He might work somewhere else and might have a life, but he has had to alter it and forget his past. This is an interesting twist, and we need to follow up to figure out the case.' I surmised.

'That is theory, Rajiv ji. How can you say only these two scenarios are possible? There could be other scenarios as well. My son can never commit this heinous crime.' Reema retorted with a protective passion in her voice. She could not agree to an explanation where we could identify her son as a murderer. Reema said they had brought him up well. She had taken care of his requirements and he displayed no psychological issues.

She continued, 'he was a cheerful kid who did not even take sides in discussions, for he felt he did not want to create any negativity in groups or in interpersonal relationships. He was a good boy with a soft heart, and he was in such happiness at having found Radha. He was so fond of her, so this was not a valid explanation. Reema told Rajiv that if he was certain of those two explanations, Reema was certain that the second explanation was bullshit. In that case, Rajiv must go after the abductors or try to find Akshay. He might be under their influence and they might have terrorized him. He might have started a life of his own in an unfamiliar environment.

As a police inspector, I knew only too well not to discount any theory, if it had a practical explanation or if it came out as a valid path, given my deductive capabilities. I needed more information. While I kept thinking about a valid motive for the crime, well, beyond the obvious rape, loot and murder, I called up my back-office guys in Latehar and Ranchi and asked them to search all the numbers that were used to call the family and to triangulate a location. That might give me the location of all the sim-cards purchased in the last ten odd days and give us enough to go after. I bade goodbye to the family and went to the airport. I could not waste any more time in Mumbai, as I had the information I so badly craved for.

CHAPTER 23

9 MARCH & 11 March 2010: 14:30 Hrs

'Sir, I think we have a new lead. You had asked us to triangulate the data that we had about the sim cards. Someone purchased all these cards at Jogbani in North Bihar.'

'I had a hunch! Give me the location or any other details that you have picked up. I would travel to Jogbani soon. If I am not mistaken, it is the northern-most part of Bihar with a border to Nepal. Nepal, as we all know, has porous borders with Bihar. People get in and get out like it is not another country but another city. Across the terai (valley) area of Nepal, Marwaris from India have set up bases and they are the main traders and businessmen. There is no difference between an Indian and a Nepali in those areas. People in those areas, like in Biratnagar, are like Biharis. Biratnagar is a large town in Nepal and is only a few kilometers from Jogbani. Jogbani is our northern-most town to have railway connectivity to the rest of India through Forbesganj and Katihar.

My hunch is and I spell it out today, our runaway boyfriend Akshay is in Biratnagar town of Nepal. He travels to Jogbani often and buys his sim cards from a particular STD booth in Jogbani. Well, Jogbani is like a tiny town with hardly much population, and I think it would not have too many booths. Let me know what we have, and I would travel tomorrow itself. That would be all.'

I think I need to inform Diya I would travel for work. It might be a couple of days. I will be out, and she might try to reach me.

'Diya, I would like to apologize as I cannot make it for our date tomorrow evening. I will travel for work. I might be back within a couple of days.'

'Inspector, that is so mean of you! You promised me after coming from Mumbai, you would spend some time with me. If before marriage itself, you are not taking me seriously, how on earth will you take care of me post marriage?' Diya had a serious tone in her voice.

'I am sorry. This travel takes me further in my investigation, and I need to hurry as we have some information now. You want me to crack this case open, right? You said so earlier in as many words, did you not?'

'Yes, my Inspector. I said so and I continue to say so. I was just joking with you. You get anxious so quickly. You need to understand me better. I am witty and you need to know me better, not only in bed but also during our conversations, my dear.'

'I agree, Diya. We need to have a good chat for a few hours, to know each other better. You know so much about me, but I know nothing about you, other than that you like me, or do you? Is that also my imagination, while you were there only for the benefits of the relationship? I hope you are not a honey trap! If you are, I am gone as I have gone bonkers, having met you and having had you as my lady love.'

'Inspector, do not go so fast. Give our relationship some time. You will understand everything and get to know me well. Now, chillax and go to your next destination. By the way, where are you traveling this time? Can I come with you? That would give me a much-needed break from Latehar, and it would give you a warm and intelligent bed–haha.'

'Not this time, Radha. I will take you the next time I travel to a wonderful location. I am going to a tiny town in North Bihar. You will not know that place and you will not wish to travel as well. There's nothing great about it.'

'Oh, so you are keeping secrets with me now! You are talking about a tiny town, but you are not telling me any names. Do you actually think I am a honey trap a.k.a. the James Bond movies?'

'Nothing like that, Diya. I will travel to Jogbani for a couple of days. That's all. Will connect with you when I can.'

'That's alright, Inspector. All the best. Get the killer and come back soon!'

11 March 2010: 14:30 Hrs

'Have you seen this boy here ever?' I asked with a display of authority. I was not alone. The STD booth guy was shell-shocked to see policemen from Jharkhand and from Bihar at his hundred square feet shop. He looked at the photo once again before denying having seen the guy. He suggested another shop nearby, inside the market area.

'Sir, I know this guy. He comes here sometimes. Am I in trouble, here?' The STD booth person enquired.

'What is your name, you piece of…' I thundered.

'Sir, I am a normal person, only trying to make a living. I am a family man. I mean no harm to anyone. This guy comes sometimes. Do I need to report whenever he comes in, next time?'

'You need to do a lot more. Tell us why he comes here and what kind of illegal trade you are doing sitting in this God forsaken shop?'

'Sir, I am an honest man. I do not deal with any illegal activities. However, some people come in and give a lot more money than normal sim card charges. This guy also comes once in a week and gives me a lot more money for the sim cards he buys from me. I take care of the paperwork and he takes it away. I now understand why he is always in a hurry. He does not wait at my shop for more than a few minutes. He comes in, gives me the money, and insists on walking out within a couple of minutes. This guy wears a sports cap of a big brand, always. Few people wear such caps here. They normally wear winter caps. He also wears a sweatshirt or a jacket with a high neck. He conceals himself well.'

'So, you are part of multiple crimes now. I hope you know that, don't you?'

'No sir, I do not take part in any criminal activities. My harmless crime is giving sim cards to people who need them. They are prepaid cards, and our telecom operators make money from these sim cards, apart from myself.'

'You are a fool of n-th order, it seems. Hope you know that only terrorists and criminals need so many prepaid cards. Normal individuals like you and me do not need prepaid cards every week. Do you have a CCTV connection here?'

'No sir, please don't do anything to me. I have young kids and family that I support. It would render them homeless without me. I do not have a CCTV connection. I never thought about it. If you so desire, I would get one installed right away. Also, next time this guy walks into my store, I would inform you immediately. He calls me a few minutes before coming here. I keep a packet of sim cards ready for him. He comes in and goes out like a breeze. As soon as I get a call from him, I would inform you.'

'That would be fine. This one time, we are leaving you. We are not taking you to prison as of now. Do your duty as a good Samaritan and no harm would come to you or to your family. By the way, when would he come over again? Any idea?'

'Sir, he would come tomorrow or the day after. It is already time. He could come today also if it is your lucky day. I would call you as soon as I get a call from him. Now, please go. If he sees police at my shop, he will never return. I do not know if he is watching.'

'Okay, on your word, we are going away. But so you know, my hawk eyes are on you. Redeem yourself, else you go to prison. No one can save you! Do you understand?'

'Very well, sir, and clearly. I have to stop selling sim cards to people who do not give their valid ID cards and I have to inform you of this gentleman as soon as I hear from him.'

I went out of the shop and asked one constable to be posted near that shop, in plain clothes. I had a feeling that we would catch hold of Akshay soon. I also had a feeling someone was watching me from close quarters. It was a bad feeling of being followed. I had to be attentive and use my reflex well. These people must be powerful, and they might try to take me out. I must be ready. It also means I am on the right track.

CHAPTER 24

17 February 2010: 06:00 Hrs (Just before the crime-one month back)

Akshay was driving Radha's father's car. It was a hatchback, and he had to pull his driving seat back to its limit. He was a tall guy, and he was used to driving sedans.

Radha noticed his discomfort and offered to drive the car. However, Akshay said he was fine, and he would maneuver it well soon. He would get used to it.

The drive from Ranchi to Netarhat is stunning. Roads are good and nature is at her best. The environs are lovely. They parked their car at multiple locations to see the beauty of the place. Jungles, valleys and hills, meandering steams; the drive had it all. They had left early, so there was not much traffic on the roads. They felt on top of the world. Their parents had agreed to their engagement and the ceremony would happen soon. They were working out the dates with priests. On Radha's insistence, Raman and Chitra allowed them to travel to Netarhat alone. They wanted to go together after a few days, but Radha insisted. She wanted to go alone with Akshay. If Radha insisted on anything, she knew, her parents would never refuse.

Raman was not quite okay with the decision, so he had allowed her for a brief stay of only two days. They had to return on the 19th.

Radha wanted to make the most of those two days. She wanted to cozy up to Akshay and possibly figure him out for herself. She wanted to know his weirdest thoughts and aspirations, his fantasies, his desires and everything crazy or nasty about him. Radha wanted to know about his family, his parents and any other person who was important to him. She wanted to be a good daughter-in-law and a dutiful wife. She wanted to open her heart to Akshay and have some of the best times of her life with him.

She knew he was head-over-heels in her love, and he wanted to have sex. She was ready as her parents had agreed to their marriage, which they will solemnize soon. Before marriage, she wanted to check her compatibility with Akshay, not only in his bed but also while staying together, in all its weird aspects. She wanted to know about his morning habits and her own acceptance of allowing someone to use her bath, and she wanted to feel him close to herself. She knew she had enough love within her, and she could keep him happy. However, she wanted not to be surprised into the relationship, post-facto. She wanted to feel it and live it before tying the knot.

They had a pleasant drive, and within four hours, they were in Netarhat. Having checked into the hotel, they went for a sumptuous brunch after a quick bath. Akshay wanted to join Radha in her bath, but she promised him a good time later. Akshay was getting crazy by the minute, and he could not keep his hands away from Radha. Even unknowingly, his hands would find her skin. She knew it intuitively, but she wanted to take it easy, nice, and slow. She knew she drove him crazy, but she wanted to know their overall compatibility.

Akshay had folded his clothes neatly and kept them inside an almirah. He did not leave his shoes near the bed. He had opened his shoes while entering the room and he had kept it in the shoe rack. Radha liked what she saw. She saw he was not being thoughtful about any of these small things; he was just being himself and she felt that his normal self was neat and clean. It comforted her in their relationship. It would have been difficult for her to stay with someone who did not believe in cleanliness. She knew most of her friends were not so tidy and they were just that way. They felt not being tidy was being manly. But where she came from, she had seen her father and her brother well behaved, and tidier than her mum.

They spent an hour having a filling and delectable lunch. Akshay wanted to have a beer, and he had one. Radha went for a soft drink. She was in no mood to go for a mocktail at that hour and felt she might just have one in the evening. She had asked the hotel to have a non-alcoholic wine sent to their room in the evening.

The day was just beginning. They went on a drive to nearby places, just around the hotel. There were few tourists, which they could clearly see. The bazaar (market area) was thinly crowded and Raman's issues with their traveling alone was not oblivious to them. They understood it was not such a great time in that part of the world and with hardly any tourists, they should not meander around till late in the day. Radha and Akshay mutually decided and went to the nearby site-seeing locations, while it was still daytime. They also thought of not going to the waterfalls in the interiors. They knew it was an amazing locale, but for their own safety, they wished not to be stupid. Akshay was happy that way as they would get more time in the confines of their bedroom, and he could utilize that time in his own passionate way.

Radha knew she could not fend off Akshay for long. She wanted to feel him and relax in his arms. They were getting into a long-term relationship and it was good that she had created this opportunity. Gods were with them, or so she felt.

They ended the day with a quick trip to the sunset point. They soaked in the lovely sight and the environs before returning to their hotel.

The hotel staff had understood it was the couple's special night. They left no stone unturned to make it big for them. When the couple returned to their room at seven in the evening, they saw their room having fresh flowers all around. It spread an aroma that took them off their feet. Radha was mesmerized by the décor and the aromatic bliss she felt being a part of. She looked appreciatively at Akshay, who did not take any credit for the show, though. He mentioned he was also amazed, and he would give a big tip to the hotel staff. The room was all decked up, and they had a non-alcoholic beverage at the table, served upfront.

There were some fresh fruits and dry fruits of all varieties. The hotel staff did the bed neatly and stocked the small refrigerator with a few beer bottles, small quarter bottles of gin, whiskey, and vodka. There were a few soda bottles and a lot of fried food to munch.

Akshay felt thrilled at the set-up in this lonely and small hill station, and he felt the people there knew a thing or two about a great evening.

While Radha went for a bath, Akshay sneaked in behind her, creating no noise, like a cat on her prowl. He held Radha from behind while she was in the shower. They were stark naked, and Radha tried to get him off, but soon she realized she had to give in. Akshay had taken a loofa in his hand, and he stroked Radha's body, creating enough foam for Radha to get rid of.

Before Radha could realize, Akshay was groaning in pleasure as he rubbed his manhood against her back. She felt him go hard and let off a painful and ecstatic groan, before suddenly going slow and spent for. While it had just begun for her, he had reached the zenith of his enraptured self.

He went out of the shower and got ready. Radha came out after ten odd minutes, wearing a white muslin robe. Akshay wore a pleasing t-shirt and shorts. He wore musk, and he was at his charming best. Akshay had already ordered some kebabs and other delicacies. He knew it was a Wednesday and Radha would love to have kebabs. The next day was a dry day for her. In his parlance, as she would not have non-veg food, it was a dry day. He wanted to make that evening special for her. While Radha got herself dressed up, the room service had already laid out the kebabs on the table, having set up their plates and cutlery. They knew the couple would not go for soups, so their tall wine glasses had liquid poured and ready.

Radha sat in front of Akshay, saying she felt loved but famished after a pleasurable experience in the bath, and she would hog it all. Akshay was apologetic at letting out steam so early, but he said he could not contain the excitement of it all. He had been waiting for that day and he got worked up. Radha told him not to worry and not to take any pressures on himself. They had an entire life to spend together, and these were silly things that he was worrying about. She was happy, and she glowed in the dim lights of their room.

Radha's charm had created a magical concoction for Akshay. He felt enamored by her lean and tall physique, her glowing skin, and her beautiful body. Her mannerisms were charming. She would roll her eyes while looking away from Akshay, who was like a student in the school, smitten and mesmerized by his teacher. Her large and luscious lips would make it increasingly difficult for Akshay to keep himself away from them. Every sip that she took, her lips would get coated with a bit of the zing from the soft drink and it would stay there for a moment too long. Akshay went bonkers, just looking at that beauty unfolding in front of him. He could see her muslin gown part slightly, midway, sometimes exposing her bedazzling beauty that he was aware was not skin deep. She was not only beautiful externally, but she had a good and clean heart and a clear conscience. Akshay would often, while having his drink, get up and come around towards Radha, kiss her on her cheeks and caress her gently. She would look at him surprised and ask him to have a fill of his favorite kebabs.

They had an extended dinner and drinks session. While Radha continued to sip on the beverage, Akshay had taken over two bottles of beer. He went to kiss Radha, suddenly, while having his drinks and food and Radha did not allow him that chance to kiss on her mouth, nicely but firmly. He understood. He had to have a clean breath before trying the act again. Akshay planned to have a good rinse of his mouth, have a couple of gums before trying it out again with Radha.

He knew Radha had some clear likes and dislikes, and he would be happy in his life with her, only if he were to follow her rules, even the smallest of them. He knew she would drive their relationship to great heights, if only he obeyed those little instructions. Best thing was, she would not say much, but her actions taught him new things about her, every day. He knew this trip was a compatibility trip for her and not so much as a pleasure trip, but he wanted to make the most of it. Akshay had a dozen crazy fantasies, and he knew he had to take it slow with her. He could not get wild unless she liked it, and he knew she would get there with some cajoling and a lot of effort. By his reading, if not cajoled, she would be a hermit in the relationship. He would not like that and hence, he had to lead the way, positively taking her places with him, in ever so gentle ways, cajoling and pushing slowly, to meet his fantasies.

It was an evening to remember for Akshay and for Radha. Akshay had used the night to get active thrice, but with a lot of alcohol in his system, his cerebrum did not help him manage coherent motion and he had reached his ecstatic state, without even reaching her truly. Radha knew it would happen someday, but she also knew Akshay had to take it slow, else he would get into a performance anxiety. She did not want him to know any of it, and she kept quiet.

Their life had just begun!

CHAPTER 25

12 MARCH 2010: 11:30 Hrs

'What is your name?' Someone in a mask asks the STD booth owner.

'Why, what happened? What is it you need?'

'Will you tell me your name, or should I just put a bullet in your head?'

'I am Bholu Ram, and I have done nothing wrong. I do not even know you. Who are you? What do you want from me? Look, I am a family man. Relax, let us first have a chat. I think you are under some confusion.'

The masked man took out a photograph that he showed to Bholu, and he showed his name written on the backside of the photograph.

Meanwhile, they heard some altercation outside. The masked man could see his friend who was waiting on a bike being questioned by someone in plain clothes. He could understand it was a policeman, by his attitude and his aggressive behavior. One could read it written all over his persona.

BAM! A loud sound of a revolver went out, tearing the small town into a stunned silence. People walking around just stopped in their tracks. The masked man came out running from the STD booth, coming close to his friend on the bike. Before the constable could react, another shot and this time again in the forehead.

The masked men zoomed away on their bikes, making sure no one followed them. Traffic around the booth stopped and people slowly found the constable and the booth owner dead. They called the ambulance, and the police.

Within minutes, I was on the spot with Raka and many constables from the nearest police station. I spoke to the bystanders, and we got to know about the unfortunate event.

I went to the booth owner's house to meet his wife and his kids. I broke the news to the family, and I saw them in a deep state of anguish for a while. It was a part of my job, but I always found it very difficult to do. For no fault of theirs, the family members of the deceased normally get their world awry and topsy-turvy within minutes. The family members had no inkling of the incoming churn for the worse in their lives. Unless it was a self-proclaimed criminal, the family members would not swallow it and they would continue to deny any ill-activity by the deceased family member.
I asked the constables to check Bholu's entire house for any leads. They got multiple mobile handsets from his cupboard. His wife was not aware of those handsets. She felt surprised, and she felt cheated by

her husband of many years. He kept those phones in switched off mode. Rajiv gave the phones to the constables and asked them to figure out the details, including all phone calls received over the last few days.

The grim turn of events nonplussed me. One murder had possibly led to another, and it was scary. We were after a larger group of people operating. It did not look like a small-town event anymore. There was a connection to Radha's case, I felt, and I knew something connected it to his visit just a day back. I thought the criminals were operating in unison and in a group; they would have involved Bholu in Radha's murder, and he was not just a person sharing sim cards with Akshay. In all this mess, I knew Akshay might be difficult to find. I asked the police to transmit Akshay's photograph at Nepal border and get him arrested while entering India whenever he comes. I was hoping it happened sooner today, as this news of the killings would spread like wildfire.

Having given my instructions to the team, I thought of going to the Nepal border. I and Raka went in a jeep towards the border.

'Sir, we have been monitoring the phone calls of people you had asked us to. We thought of reporting one activity to you. We heard a different phone call from the Bangalore kid Ravi. Someone spoke to him, checking about their health and their well-being. The other person asked about Ravi and Saurav. He seemed to know them. From Ravi's voice, we think he did not recognize the caller. He was not expecting a call from an unknown caller, who knew about both

Saurav and him. However, he said they were just about ok, and they used to miss Radha. The gentleman on the call knew Radha, it seemed, from a pause that he took before telling Ravi that he would find suitable brides for them, before bidding his goodbye.' It was Pradeep from Latehar.

I was mulling over my options. I wanted to get back to the confines of my room and map the information, as I knew getting hold of Akshay was important. We could not leave it to chance. The October 2, 1953, extradition treaty between Nepal and India was archaic but available. I did not want to get into any issues with the extradition treaty. That would set his investigation back by months. I was fully aware today was an important day in this investigation, and I had to be available at the border to nab Akshay.

'Sir, we saw the guy you were looking for. When he saw us looking at his photograph, he ran back towards the border. Before we could apprehend him, he crossed over to the other side of the border and stood there, looking at us. He has definitely understood we are looking for him. We have not crossed to the other side of the border. As police, we cannot go to that side of the border. What do you want us to do now?'
'That's terrible. I have been looking for him for long. He knows you will not cross over to Nepal, but he must be around that area to figure out why he was being searched. He might be still there in that area. I am getting there within a few minutes. I can cross over to Nepal, as I am in plain clothes. Just monitor Akshay. Keep tracking him using binoculars. Well, I can see you. Let me come over to you.'
'Hello, I am Rajiv and I can see Akshay. He looks

worried, but he is still not sure whether the police were looking for him. He is sitting in a restaurant near the border, sipping tea, monitoring movement on this side of the border. I will go there. Give me a bike that doesn't look like a police vehicle.'

'Sir, please take this bike. This is my personal bike. Here are the keys. Let me know if you need any weapon.' Constable asked.

'Thank you for all help. I will get back within half an hour, maybe less. Raka, please cover for me, if required. Get over to the other side of the border quickly if you see any distress signs. I hope he will not take any counter measures, as he seems to be a white collar kid. I need to take my chances here.'

'We will monitor the situation from here, boss. I will come over on another bike, if required. You go ahead, before he moves out, back towards Nepal.' Raka mentioned.

Within minutes of crossing over to the Nepal side of the border, I reached the restaurant. I parked my bike outside and took a seat near Akshay's. I ordered a tea for myself. I felt Akshay was tense, and he was perspiring. He was aware Indian police were after him and he was thinking of getting out of his troubles somehow. I went near him and sat in a seat next to him. I murmured in a low voice that he was under arrest and he should not create any scene. I saw a terrified expression on his face. I quickly showed him my ID, and I told him he had nowhere else to go. If he did not give in, we would arrest him in public. That would create a lot of nuisances and they would shame him in public. He looked like a decent criminal, but it was difficult these days to figure out anyone. I prepared for the worst and I hoped he did not run away from there, making me go after him in a goose chase, complicating matters with Nepal police. He, however, decided against any creative measures and cooperated immediately. I took him to my bike and brought him over to the Indian side of the border, with little ado.

I do not wish to take Akshay to the police station. Rather, let me take him to my guest house. I need to inform my counterpart of the same and I will assure him I would hand him over if he had a role to play in the entire events unfolding. I requested for only a day to detain Akshay in my own way. My counterpart was aware of some good work that I was doing for the department, and he meant no harm. He wished to extend all help required. I was happy policemen at my level were cooperative.

'Akshay, let us have lunch. I do not wish to detain you, but I need answers. So, we would stay together for tonight with no police around. Do not forget, I am a cowboy myself, so no hanky-panky. Deal?'

'Yes.' Akshay murmured.

We had a decent lunch in utter silence. I hope to uncover the truth while Akshay expected to get back to his home.

'Now, talk!'

'I have nothing to say, and I have lost my world, literally and figuratively. I lost my girlfriend, and I lost my life as I used to live. I had to change my life to the life of a wanderer who could not even speak to his parents. They gave her hell, and they are giving me hell, now.'

'Can we talk about them? Who are they? Why did they do what they did to you and to Radha?'

'I know nothing about them. They were powerful people. I do not know why they chose us. All I know is they found us meandering in that area behind the hutments. We had gone there to pick some beautiful flowers. I knew Radha loved flowers, and that area was full of a large variety of species. We were being cautious; therefore, we did not go out of Netarhat town. We did not go to any falls or anywhere else. We wanted to just feel the location and get back to our lives.'

I extended a glass full of water towards Akshay. Akshay was perspiring, thinking about the worst day of his life, feeling the same pain he had felt, and the pain he saw Radha feel that day.

'Rajiv sir, we saw some people suddenly appear from the hutments and move towards us. We felt suspicious, and we started moving back towards the road. Before we could have got back on the road, they ran towards us and apprehended us. They showed us our photos and told us not to worry as they were there for help, and they meant no harm. They surprised us by showing our snaps on them, but we also felt Radha's parents might have sent them for our safety purpose; as Radha's dad was not happy about our visit alone at the location. He had given in to the demands of his daughter, but probably, he was being cautious.

So, we went with them, without raising a hue and cry, right inside a hutment. What we saw was a small room with some utensils in a side kitchen. There was nothing else and the hut owner must have been living in penury. It surprised us why Radha's dad would use such people for our protection, and then we suddenly realized these people had lied to us. I looked at Radha and we tried to run out of the hut. Before we could do so, we saw another guy at the door. He pushed us in and then it went from bad to worse. They tied my hands after seating me on a chair, towards my back.

What they did to Radha was incomprehensible. To my utmost horror, they started stripping Radha of her clothes. There were two of them, a lady who was old and a well-built guy. Radha tried to fight back and kicked the guy in his groin. That guy was in pain for a while, but he soon recovered and tied her legs on the bed. All this while, that old hag had Radha under her control. Her strength and her conviction surprised me, as she had held on to a girl possibly half her age and someone who was taller and better built. The old lady dominated Radha.

After tying Radha to the bed, they cut whatever was left of her clothes on the body. They put a cloth in her face, which almost choked her. She could not talk or could not call out loudly. They had already stuffed my mouth as well. They allowed me to see the proceedings as it unfolded in front of me, to my utter horror. So, they did not allow us even a moment to question why we were there in such a position or what they wished to do to Radha or to me. I could not see Radha any more in that state, and I closed my eyes for a bit. Suddenly, the door flung open, and I opened my eyes to see another young guy enter the room.

Meanwhile, I saw the lady decorating the room with incense sticks and flowers. She had also prepared the room for prayers. It amused me unendingly. I felt sick to my gut, and I could only see Radha in her utter state of shock. I felt guilty and sad at having brought her to Netarhat in the first place and having got off the main road to a side area of the hutments, just to pluck a few flowers. I could never have realized there was so much danger lurking within the area, and one slight mistake did us in.

There was no way to get out of the rope tied to my hands and to my feet. I could not do much, other than cry with eyes wide open, hoping against hope for a classic intervention of the merciful Gods. While I looked for mercy and Radha hoped for it as well, we suddenly saw the guy who had come into the room later, open his clothes. I squirmed, hoping this was not an attempt to rape Radha. As another lady was in the room, I thought that would not happen, and I prayed for mercy from the Gods.

As luck or ill-luck would have it, the three of them spoke to one another in some other language that I did not understand, and then the lady and the other guy left the room and went outside. The lady did not like it and she made her dislike obvious by hitting her head hard by her palm, but still she went out. Now, this guy was there, alone, with us. He took out a blade from somewhere and he gave himself a few cuts in quick succession. He was in utter pain, and it nauseated me for a moment, having looked at blood oozing out of his fresh wounds. It bewildered me as I kept thinking about the man who could inflict such pain on himself, then what he could do to us.

He then lost his cloth in a jiffy, including the bare minimums and climbed on to the bed, over Radha. I knew what happened in front of me and I just hoped it would end soon. She was in utter pain during her rape, and I could do nothing. He was in a seance of sorts and looked taken over by some spirits or something unknown to me. Was it an evil spirit or a ghost or an evil eye or something I did not know of? When his pleasure ended, tears covered Radha's face, and she had an empty look in her eyes. Her eyes were asking multiple questions, and I did not have any answers. I know she asked me what happened to my manliness and why I could not save her. I know she was angry at me. After all of this, however, I still had a hope that they would allow us to leave, after a warning or something of that sort. We would have gone back to our lives and while it would have shaken and stirred our relationships, it would still have prevented the unfortunate events that followed. Once the guy got done with the act of raping her, he allowed the old hag and the other guy to get into the room. Then I saw the old lady take out ghee, and she started putting it all over Radha's body. It took me sometime to understand what was going on, but I understood she was being prepared for a sacrifice.

At this, I started jumping on my chair and the chair itself gave in and I fell to the floor. My hands were tied at my back, so before I could do something, the two guys took control over me and pushed me out of the hut to another hut in the vicinity. They tied me there and one guy stayed in my hut. The other two people were with Radha. I could only imagine what happened to her thereafter. I had no chance of seeing her again. While I was waiting for the bad news to come, the guy in my room started hyperventilating and he took out a blade as well. He gave me some sharp cuts through my shirt. I was in utmost pain, and I went blank after that. I came back to my senses after a while, and I realized what had just happened.

The three of them were standing in front of me, and all of them had blood on them. I could see sharp cuts on their bodies as well. So, this had something to do with their beliefs and rituals. I could understand. They had auspicious red and yellow marks on their heads and blood on their bodies. They were also carrying incense sticks in their hands. The two guys looked thrilled, and the lady looked like she had won a prize or something. I understood little, but I was a worried man.

By their looks, I knew I had lost Radha, and it was my turn. I cursed them without a sound in my mouth. It hurt badly.

The lady spoke to me in measured words, not in the Hindi language that I know, but I understood what she said. She told me they had to take Radha's life as she was a pure soul, and it was, as per their religious beliefs and practices. However, they did not want me to meet the same fate and they would free me soon.

She also told me I should vanish and not get back to my family or to my people. She told me they had a big cult called Snake Charmers, and they were almost omnipresent. If I were not to listen to them and if I tried to speak to anyone about whatever happened that day, they would get me killed. I knew she was not talking rubbish. She was almost meditating and talking with a purpose I had not seen in others. She looked like a messenger of the unworldly powers, and all this scared the hell out of me. I had lost Radha, but the ugly and selfish me wanted to survive. I have a survivor's guilt now, but I did what I was told.

They took my bloodied shirt away and gave me an old and dirty shirt to wear. Then they handed me over to another guy who then brought me over two days to Jogbani. That guy is the owner of an STD booth in the town area. I go to meet him once every week as I had promised to them, and I also take multiple sim cards from him. That way I stay in touch with my parents, but I do not speak to them. That way, they have kept me safe and they are also safe.

Now that you have apprehended me, the entire mystery is out in the open and you know about me. They would get me killed. I am worried. That STD booth owner would get me killed,' saying thus, Akshay sobbed.

'If you can catch hold of that guy, Bholu, at the booth, he would tell you all about the murderers of Radha. I hope you catch him fast, else if he knows you have taken me in, they will try to kill me.'

'Hold on, Akshay. I have some news for you. They have killed Bholu today, a couple of hours back. Two masked men got to him before we could save him. It was a daylight killing, and they have killed one of my constables also, who was there in plain clothes. So, we have little of clues left, anyway. What else can you tell us?' Rajiv asked.

'Oh God! See, they are so powerful. They would get me killed also wherever you take me. They are omnipresent, as that lady had told me. I do not want to die. I want to go back to Mumbai and stay with my parents. Can you do that, Rajiv sir?'

'Give me some time, Akshay. I need to think about what is happening. What is this group, Snake Charmers, and why did they plan these gruesome murders? You yourself are not out of my watch, and while you have told me a good cover story, I am not fully convinced. So, better watch out! If there are any loopholes in the story, I would get you sent to the Andaman black site and you would never get back here.'

Akshay squirmed and sat back in his bed. I told him to relax while he could, and I got back to my phone calls.

I called up Pradeep in Latehar and told him to keep a track of all the incoming and outgoing calls of the subjects I had asked him to bug. I had a feeling they would hear something from someone that would help my understanding of the developing situation. I knew the group of killers were dangerous, and I was in danger. I was also thinking how this so-called omnipresent group found my scent so quickly. They did not take a minute to figure out my location. Was it Diya? No, it can't be. I am just being a stupid Inspector and having doubts over the only good thing that has happened to me in my life.

I thought of having a chat with my teacher, an old Professor of anthropology, Dr. M. Tiru. Dr. Tiru used to stay in Muzaffarpur, so I thought of traveling to the town. I knew it would be worth my time, as I would get a clear understanding of what I was up against. Professor could help me if there was anything related to people and societies, sects, and cults. Dr. Tiru had a great understanding of the masses in Bihar and Jharkhand, and his words of wisdom would help me deduce further in his case. I handed over Akshay to the local police and asked them to keep him for just one more day. I would take care of Akshay after returning from Muzaffarpur.

CHAPTER 26

13 March 2010: 13:00 Hrs

Guys, I am time, and I am back again.

No one knows the life and times of these three musketeers better than me. I know every minute of your existence as well, but do not feel spooky. It is not like someone is watching over you. This one is existential, and you do not worry about the same.

Saurav was in his bedroom, lying prostate on the floor, naked. He had bolted the door from inside and he had told Mr. Murali to prepare lunch that he would not have before two o'clock. Saurav was in a trance, or so it seemed. He was murmuring verses, and it was not in his normal language, Hindi. It might have been in his native language. I do not know as I do not want to keep an audit of even the languages that people speak. I am happy knowing who does what, with their precious time and having seen Saurav in this unique position, I knew he was up to something that he would not reveal to his friends or relatives.

This was unique to him, and he had done it a few times in the past as well. He had a distinct tattoo on his bare chest, and it was of an eagle being killed by a dagger, pointing right at the eagle's eye, with a drop of blood oozing out of the eagle's eye. It was a ghastly and gory tattoo, and anyone might have puked, having taken a sudden look at something like that. With multiple sharp cuts and wounds on his body, I did not understand how Saurav expected any girl worth her salt to like him, leave alone Radha? I had no answers, but I knew I would see what happens next.

To make things simple, I have been privy to this act not only from Saurav but also from a distinct set of people. They do not live in Jharkhand alone. They stay across the globe, and they unite in this activity at least once in a year. Not all of them would be present for this activity, the same day. This cult of believers conducts such activities regularly and the believers must be a part of at least one such activity once a year.

Saurav turned in a simple harmonic motion but continued to be in a trance. After some time, he sat up and took out some auspicious substances, and put it over his body, including on his forehead, for some religious requirement. Thereafter, he took out a sharp blade and looked at his body. His body had undulations in multiple places. He found a clean spot and dug the blade in, creating a sharp cut, and blood oozed out. Saurav writhed in pain but waited for some blood to flow out before trying to close the wound with a medical gauge. He applied some medicine and then got up. He went to his attached bath, cleaned himself up and took a warm water bath. Thereafter, Saurav applied the medicine and gauge once again. He sat in front of his Gods and got into another session of deep prayers and chanting, all in a low voice; lest Mr. Murali would have heard him.

I piqued me, at people who gave themselves such pain and suffering, knowingly, in the name of customs or religion. I would never understand people. Anyway, I have a lot of work to do as I keep time for the universe. What I noticed is Saurav was throughout connected via his mobile video app to a large group of people, throughout performing his prayers. I felt it was a religious sect that had a different approach to being than the normal Hindu way or anything that I have seen across other religions. I know such unique sects or cults, or secret societies operate across the world and the number of people who take part in such activities is not much, it is but a drop in an ocean; but these people were committed to their sects, and they go to extreme ends to protect their identities.

Some of these sects give instructions to carry out harmful activities in the name of protecting their religion or that of their sects, and the followers considered such instructions coming from the top as a supreme order.

Saurav was one such follower, and he waited for his call. He was a genuinely good person, but he would do whatever was told to him, like a loyal soldier of the cult. Even his parents were not aware of him being in the secret cult.

CHAPTER 27

13 March 2010: 15:00 Hrs (Same day)

Pradeep told me about Saurav, that he got a phone call from someone who showed an urgency in his voice. They summoned him to Muzaffarpur, a district in Bihar.

I asked two of my team members to be ready to tail Saurav, from Patna airport. They had his photograph, and they knew Saurav would travel to Patna the next day. We also knew from the phone call Saurav would remain discreet and not report this matter to anyone, including to his parents. The constables hearing the taped message felt Saurav was excited to hear the news and possibly excited he would travel to Muzaffarpur. I was happy I was traveling to Muzaffarpur to meet Dr. Tiru anyway and I will welcome Saurav, there.

Soon, they could find out that Saurav had used his credit card to buy a flight ticket. They found out his flight details from the airline.

I reached Dr. Tiru's house at 7 pm the same evening. I had with me a small briefcase having my nightgown and other belongings. I had already booked a room in the police guest house for the night.

'Dr. Saheb (Sir), how have you been? It has been a long time that we have not met.'

'I am good. It is great to meet one of my best students, ever. Yes, that is correct. I have produced many an academician and have produced at least forty anthropologists who have done multiple types of research under me, but I have produced one such person in you, Rajiv, I am truly proud of. In you, I have produced the finest student of the studies in the human way of life, and you are a practising member. Few people use this knowledge practically, but I know it helps you with your deduction process. Eventually, a human mind is complex. Oh, sorry, I was so happy to see you I did not even ask you for a coffee. Would you have a black coffee or my type of milk coffee?' Dr. Tiru asked Rajiv.

While sipping our cream coffee, we had a long conversation. I narrated the entire case history of Radha and my predicament at not being able to find a motive.

'Rajiv, I guess you are correct. If I am right, this is a very simple case. A cult member or members who wanted to protect themselves from the wrath of the almighty caught Radha for the sacrifice. It was seemingly their best way to indulge in the act of a human sacrifice. Because of one of their own acts, they might have felt they had attracted the wrath of the Gods and therefore, the best way to appease the Gods and their dead ancestors was through the sacrifice of a pure soul. In Radha, they got that pure soul who they could sacrifice at His altar. They could have also done it to negate the effects of the illness of the old hag, as you mentioned earlier. Her sons might have committed this act to please the Gods and in doing so, they would have thought their mother's health would improve.

I can tell you one more thing here, Rajiv. These people might not be people of a particular class or caste. They can be people you or I know, and those people might move in our midst. That is one reason we did not find those people. They were not locals at all. They were not from Netarhat, else, by now your team would have traced them. Even the local villagers would have handed them over to you, by now.'

'Dr. Tiru, then why did they leave Akshay and did not harm him, other than, of course, giving him a few sharp cuts on his body? Why was he spared? Is two not better than one, as a sacrificial lamb? Would Gods not be happier?'

'No, Rajiv, killing is a sin, and that this so called Snake Charmers cult also knows. One killing, done in the proper way following all relevant rituals, is a sacrifice. Two is a killing spree, and it is not acceptable in even archaic religions or beliefs. Had it been cannibalism or headhunting of any sort, in those few tribes that might exist even now, they would not spare either Akshay or Radha, and you would not have even found their bodies. So, I am clear in my mind this is a propitiatory offering to the Almighty and nothing more.'

'Dr. Tiru, how can you explain rape of the girl prior to the sacrifice?'

'I have no explanation for that, Rajiv. No sect would allow the sacrificial being to go through a rape before the offering. A rape prior to a sacrifice depicts a crooked and a dirty mind of a sexual predator and of a pervert. That is one reason the mother might not have wanted her son to do what he did, which Akshay felt he understood from their talks. However, obviously the youngster wanted his self-aggrandizement before the sacrifice, and the others allowed, grudgingly.'

'So, would you know any groups that practise such an extreme form of worship involving human sacrifice? As far as I am aware, in the entire world today, it is a crime. In all religions, killing human beings is a crime. Is it some nomadic tribes that still practise such acts?'

'Rajiv, I have answered this question already while I was summing up the case. There could be powerful cults with multiple members across the world. However, one practise is common to all cults. They would have a specific ritualized routine of offering their prayers to their deity. They would practise the form in communions and prayer meetings. Nowadays, with technology, they might practise it using mobile phones or whatever. I am personally not privy to any such group as having an information of such a group and not reporting it to the law enforcement agencies, by itself, is unlawful.'

'Do you think Dr. Saheb, that these people could be violent jihadis or Naxalite with left leanings?'

'Do not color your thoughts so much, Rajiv. This is a simple case. This is the work of an active cult that believes in human sacrifice. You could not distinguish them from ourselves, as they could be distinguished members of our society. They could be ministers, IAS officers, judges and jury members. It would be impossible to weed it out, and I think it will be like a large body with tentacles spread across the world. This cult will not have tribals alone. It would have believers in every caste, creed, and nationality. They would have a guru, a teacher in whom everyone would have extreme faith.'

'I understand, Dr. Tiru. I had one more question. Akshay had said that their photograph was already there with those people who showed it to them and took them to their hut. How could they have their photograph?'

'That is an interesting fact, Rajiv, and that is also a clue to your case itself. Their guru has ordered this act of sacrifice for one of the cult members. So, if I think I understand it fully, I surmise that someone from the cult might be in a one-sided relationship with the girl, or it might have been some other reason as well. But one member of the cult had a harrowing time because Radha was getting betrothed to Akshay. Was it Ravi or was it Saurav? Who do you think loved her more or wanted to be with her for his life?'

'Dr. Tiru, from my personal understanding of the situation, it was Saurav. So, do you think Saurav has got something like this done to the person he loved the most in his life? Would he go to such levels to prove a point? Would he be a conspirator in taking away the life of his beloved, if she were to marry someone else, while she waited for him for over a year? This is confusing and, to my mind, impossible. Saurav would do nothing like this.'

'You are right there, Rajiv. It is not Saurav. However, it can be people who love Saurav. If Saurav is a member of the secret cult and someone they love, as a group member, any of the other group members could do it for him, in the name of preserving the equanimity of the cult. Imagine having a member who gets disturbed every time he sees his girlfriend with another guy. As a powerful sect, the guru might give a kill order without Saurav even knowing anything about it. Do you think so?'

'Oh, my God! That can happen, rather than anything else happening, when we are talking about a private membership based secret society where people are believers and followers, and the wrath of the guru runs supreme. Guru is drunk on his powers, and he can take steps that you and I cannot even imagine. In his own idiosyncratic and dogmatic ways, he might have ordered this kill, just to protect a believer from a constant source of sadness.'

'I think we are on the right path. Saurav would give you the key to this entire episode. You can verify it easily as Saurav's body would have multiple, self-inflicted wounds made by a sharp object. His body would have distinct undulations. He might also have a specific mark or tattoo on his body. Trust you to understand how we have deducted a complex problem using simple deduction techniques. You could have deduced it yourself, but it is easier when two people talk it out, together.'

'Yes, Dr. Saheb, thanks a lot! I will get cracking. I need to get to Saurav anyhow and fast. Let me check him out. Do you think there could be any other way this entire drama could have unfolded?'

'No, I think we have the answer in front of us. Go after Saurav. Let him lead and you might uncover an enormous story with powerful people behind covers. Be very careful with your life as these people would go to any lengths to protect their identities. They can get you killed if they feel you would uncover their secrets. They can be ruthless, and they have multiple kill agents. So, be wary and go, and I prepared myself to stay there for a few days, to get behind Saurav. The cat-and-mouse chase had begun.

CHAPTER 28

14 March 2010: 14:00 Hrs

'Sir, we have lost Saurav. We were just behind him while maintaining our normal tailing distance. Suddenly, a truck overtook us and in a split-second, we could not find Saurav in the car. The car was stranded on the road-side kerb and the inmates, including the driver, were not there. We searched the area, but we could find no one. No one has claimed the car yet.'

'Oh God! You guys should have gone after the truck. The truck guys would have picked up Saurav, from what I understand from your description. Did the truck stop ahead of you even for a moment?' Rajiv enquired.

'Yes sir, the truck had abruptly stopped just ahead of us, blocking our view, but by the time we could react, they went away.'

'Do you have the truck's plate? Share it with me.'

'No sir, we did not figure out it was the truck, so we did not take its number. It has been only a few minutes, and we are at toll 21. The next police check-post could apprehend them if they are aware. So, let me just inform them right away.' The constable kept the phone.

I spoke to the police check-post after a while, and I got to know they had apprehended two trucks before the constables reached the post. Both the trucks had only a driver and a help. They did not have anyone else. I knew it was a big game, and that I was behind the curve. They have whisked Saurav into another car before the police check-post. I knew criminal minds were beautiful, and they used a lot of gray matter. I had to up my game if I were to understand the developing story. Media had already categorized the case as an epic failure of the police, and I was collecting a lot of bad name.

It is important to redeem myself. How can I find Saurav? I knew any future clue would present itself through Saurav, Ravi or through their parents. I once again checked whether my team was going through the transcript of all the tapped phone calls. I released Akshay, and I sent him with a constable to Mumbai. I told Akshay to speak to me every few days, so I knew he was in Mumbai and safe and he had received no questionable calls, or no one had approached him at his residence. I had advised Akshay not to roam around the city and to stay back home for his own safety.

My Latehar police team transmitted me news that Ravi spoke to his parents that evening and he spoke about not being able to connect with Saurav. He hoped Saurav was well, and it was just a dead battery issue with his hand phone. It was clear Ravi was not aware of the unplanned trip of Saurav.

I had an ominous feeling about the entire episode. I had to figure out a way to find out Saurav, soon, else it would be too late. The case would be closed for want of evidence and I would get egg on my face for supervising a case that the police could never solve. I knew the entire department would try to protect the super powerful people involved in this case, but I had to find a way.

As providence would have it, Saurav's parents got a call from an unknown number, and they were disturbed by the caller. The caller informed them that their son got married to a beautiful girl from North Bihar and their son- and daughter-in-law would meet them in a couple of days. The caller introduced himself and told Saurav's parents not to report the case to the police. Else, they would never see their son, ever again.

I knew Saurav got married against his will after an act of abduction, and it was quite common in that part of Bihar, even up to a few years back. However, I felt it was a different turn of events, and I expected nothing like this to happen. Either the criminal mind behind all this was adept at stage managing the show, he was being two steps ahead of me, or there was some issue in the construct of my assessment of the situation. It might just be that Dr. Tiru had based his theory on a false premise, and the truth was totally different.

I was nonplussed, and I needed a drink down my scorched throat. I went to a nearby drunkard's den and ordered whiskey on the rocks. I enquired the bartender about such marriages through abductions and the bartender said such things were not happening anymore. If something like that had happened recently, it will surprise the locals too. He also said that if it has happened, the girl side would be infamous and very strong, and the guy should just accept his fate. Any act of running away from the marriage would mean death and nothing else. They will destroy his family. With a few notes to grease the process, and upon sufficient insistence, I got a couple of names of big men in the city who had the power to do such a thing.

I put a couple of constables outside the houses of the few people whose names I had just heard. I had a feeling we will go some distance with this changed approach and we might get the details of Saurav's abductors soon. This was a calculated risk, as it would annoy those powerful people if they got to know about our surveillance. We were going on a presumption, with no evidence. They could take the police to the courts, and it could destroy my career. However, something told me it was only a matter of time. I was thinking to myself, while having a drink and choicest dry chilli chicken, that the case was of a big canvas and I had limited resources at my command. However, I was happy that my senior had allowed me complete freedom and a lot of leverage. I hoped I would crack the case and it would happen soon.

While having the drink, I felt someone watching me. The feeling was like the earlier occasion, while I was in Jogbani. I was in danger, and I had to keep my reflexes active. This drinking could get me killed. I stopped drinking, picked up a couple of chicken chilli pieces, chewed them fast and got up. I went up to the counter, made my payment and checked with the person whether he knew who was following me, in a very hushed tone. All he said was I need to be careful around there and rush back to safety of my guest house.

I got out and went towards my jeep. The driver was not around and just as I took out my phone to call him, I suddenly saw a shadow behind me. The clothing looked like that of a girl. I turned, a little flustered, but there was no one there. I looked over, moved around further in that area, and tried to search for the person. I suddenly saw Diya just around the corner, getting into an alley and getting lost. Was it Diya? Was I dreaming or was I fully drunk? What would she do in Muzaffarpur? I called my driver, gave him instructions to follow my lead. I ran towards the alley, half-suspecting dangers lurking in the alleys. As soon as I reached the alley, while I could hear my jeep getting started, someone hit me on my head with a blunt object. Before I could realize anything, I went blank. I opened my eyes later, in a hospital. My driver was sitting there, waiting for me to get up. He called the doctor on duty, who checked me, asked me a few questions, and asked the nurse to take me for a CT scan.

They processed the reports and got back to me over the next few hours. I got to know from the driver that when he entered the alley; he found me on the road, holding my head and passed out. My head was a bit swollen, so he could figure out someone hit me. He took me back to safety and saved my life.

He checked my dress, but he found nothing on me. There was no clue, no external paper, no warning letters, nothing. I asked for my mobile and tried calling Diya. Her phone rang fully, but she did not pick it up. It was 4 am, and it was now 15th March.

I was nowhere near any breakthrough and my life as I knew it with Diya was already in big trouble.

I called up Pradeep and asked him to find out the Diya's location, through her phone. While I was mulling my options, I got to know that Diya's phone was at Latehar, but she was not picking it up. Did I really see Diya? Is she in Muzaffarpur? Is she following me? Has she come close to me only to get the internal details of my investigation? This case is getting interesting! These are serious people, and it is a big fish. They have multiple powers, and they are using every trick in the trade to keep me away and foxed. I need to figure this out. It may just be that they planted Diya to get feedback of my travel schedules, et al. That would always give them a leverage, and I would circle around with no real clues. They take out all the clues that I find, and they also take out all the people I find even remotely involved. They keep cleaning their slate while committing new crimes, and I am nowhere near finding the truth. I go around in circles and they eventually take away the case from me. The case would get closed for good, with no evidence, as an unsolvable case; and I lose my dignity as a detective.

I cannot let this happen. I cannot let my personal relationships come in the way of my being able to solve this case. I must keep away from Diya, from booze, and keep focused, so I solve this problem. I need to keep a safe distance from Diya for the time being and I can be blunt, saying I am busy, and I don't have any me-time as of now. My job is on the line, and I need to protect my name and my integrity. Let personal relationships go to hell!

There were multiple questions in my activated brain. It seems the impact on my head had activated hitherto dormant nerves in my brain, creating new connections, activating a barrage of activity. I was suddenly working on multiple angles and different scenarios. One aspect was clear, that I had to keep away from Diya for some time and I had to keep my movements completely secret. I was being tailed, and I had to fix those guys. I was also waiting for some information from the constables whom I had deputed outside the bungalows of big guys of the city.

CHAPTER 29

15 March 2010: 15:00 Hrs

I was at a nearby police station in Muzaffarpur town. I waited to hear some news about Saurav, and I felt I was getting impatient. I could not sit in Muzaffarpur for an eternity, trying to figure out Saurav's whereabouts. His parents had not even reported his missing case in the police, and they had accepted their fait accompli. They had to welcome Saurav and his wife. I knew Saurav could have had Radha, if he had accepted her proposal in time and there he was at a different time, wherein these goons did not even allow him his choice. He had to marry someone out of the blue with a gun's barrel down his throat. I said to myself, 'give me a break!'

I was now under pressure I had not felt before. I knew this group of people were powerful and the nearer I reached to cracking the case, the more I would disturb their equanimity and the more they would resolve to kill me. I could not believe in any one person within the police force also, as it would be very difficult to figure the people involved. I was not aware who could pass on all my information. I had to keep all the information close to myself, without letting other people in on my deduction. I also thought of calling Pradeep from Latehar. Raka and Pradeep were my closest and I would be better around them, well, hopefully, unless one of them were sold to the powers that be.

I also felt I should ease out a bit and relax like the other policemen in a case. That might give me new insights after all. I wanted to soothe my nerves. I knew I had to take it easy, and an early opportunity would present itself as a gift. Well, if only it was so easy in life. There is nothing worse for a detective than to rely on a hint or a clue that comes forward naturally, like a gift from gods. One must help oneself deduct and figure out the possibilities. We must thoroughly analyze a game of probabilities and any options that get thrown up.

While I was mulling over the probabilities, I got the news of a sighting of Saurav in a mansion in the heart of the town. I went there with a large police team, supported by commandos. I knew the mansion would have gunmen, and I had to be prepared for any eventuality. My counterpart had been kind to have organized a quick search warrant signed by a magistrate. We armed ourselves to the teeth, and we went for the kill. We raided the mansion and within minutes, while my team held the owner of the property at gunpoint, we found Saurav and his wife in a room on the third floor. Saurav was sleeping after a sumptuous lunch, I was told. He was enjoying the fruits of his marriage, even though it was a forced one and he was making the most of the opportunity.

They brought Saurav downstairs where I was standing. Before Saurav could realize, in a flash, I cut through the t-shirt that Saurav was wearing. I found a symbol on his chest, marked by a dagger in an attacking position, and a drop of blood oozing out of the eye of an eagle. I also saw his body had multiple wounds, and he was a practitioner of sorts. Or a believer, whatever you say. Before anyone could realize what suddenly happened, I sprang and cut open the kurta of Saurav's father-in-law. The gentleman had the same mark on his chest and multiple wound marks on the entire body. The police apprehended Saurav and his father-in-law. His father-in-law was gregarious and he was full of himself. This raid was a swift one and it yield the right dividends to my case. I knew we had just had our first big breakthrough in the case, and it was something to chew upon and move forward.

We presented both Saurav and his father-in-law, Rajveer Singh, to the magistrate the same evening, and took him on a fourteen-day police remand.

I felt I was near the truth, and that we would figure it out soon. I knew Rajveer was a local tough man, and it would be difficult to hold him for long. I had to get the truth from the father-in-law and son-in-law duo before they get a fast one up on me.

I also knew they represented the lower end of the spectrum possibly, and there were stronger people, higher up the cult chain of command. By now I was aware I was a small fry and that I was on to something bigger than myself, and the stroke of a pen could derail my entire investigation mighty quick. My case could go away from me or I they may transfer me. They may even kill me at the slightest provocation.

I thought of speaking to my journalist friend and to confide into her, before anything happened to me. I wanted to have a preventive and selective leak to the media.

CHAPTER 30

16 March 2010: 15:00 Hrs

I was all over the local press the other day. I had given bits and pieces of information to the press and my investigation had become the talk of the town. Rajveer and Saurav had become the talk of the state and they had become infamous.

I had kept a lot of information to myself, and I had not put out the facts about the Snake Charmers cult in the open. I had, however, revealed that I had secrets to keep for a few days and that I would get out with it soon. The press had also mentioned that there had been an attempt to my life, and either a transfer or a normal-looking accident could neutralize me sooner that people could realize. I almost immediately had an upper hand because of this selective press release and he was one up in this game, over the powers that be, in the cult hierarchy.

The press was already talking about a breakout of Rajveer, from police custody, by minister level people, and it gave the goons a medicine in their own method.

I knew I had prevented the cult from taking any hasty decisions in neutralizing the investigation by any easily understood method and I knew the state police chief would not want to go on record immediately, by shifting me out of the case. That would have looked silly, and no state police chief wanted to look like a fool to the crowd of his state.

With time on my side, I investigated Saurav and Rajveer separately and recorded the two sessions, for a better understanding of the unfolding situation, and of truth.

'Rajveer ji, hope my guys have taken good care of you? Did you get your biryani this afternoon? You are a famous man in the country. Everyone knows your name now. So much for being infamous!'

'What do you want from me, Rajiv? Why did you get me here? What is your charge? Why am I here? I am not a terrorist; then how can you detain me? My lawyers are moving the courts today and I would get out soon. Let me out nicely and I would take care of you. I would not go after you, and I would not be a reason for your future troubles. I know you have had a troubled past. I know everything about you, Rajiv. Rajiv, I know you have had a troubled childhood. You were with parents who did not see eye-to-eye. You were always afraid of their fights and lies and deceit. They had very different lives, and you were caught in a bad family. I know everything about you, Rajiv. Shall I keep talking?'

'Oh, I did not realize you are a psychologist, too. I am impressed. You are correct in your facts about my childhood. However, this does not mean you have mapped me for good. I mean, I am a man of steel and I have come up in life the hard way. I am not prepared to let go just because a petty goon from Muzaffarpur thinks he can get the better of me. You want to pull a prank on me? Go on! What more do you know about me? Let us talk business, else, let me tell you, once and for all, I would give you hell!'

'You police guys are almost always drunk on your power and your position. I hope you know you guys are egotistic, but you do not know who I am. Are you even aware that the Bihar DGP comes and sits on my verandah while I am inside, getting a massage? I am *Bahubali*, do you understand–a muscle man! People take my name with awe and with fear in this part of the world and from where you come, I can run my writ there as well. So, let me give you a piece of advice, and I can tell you for a fact, no police protection would help you. No commando force can save you from my wrath. Do not take it too far. I know you are from outside this area, and you had no clue while you came into my house to get me. Now that you know about me, leave me now. Also leave my son-in-law.'

'Funny, is it not? He is now your son-in-law by force! It is natural that you had to get one by force, as no one would have married into your family by choice. Look what kind of life you have given to your daughter. I can't imagine what kind of life you have given to your spouse. Tell me, when both of you are from the same cult, why did you have to abduct Saurav to get your daughter to marry him? You could have even got your guruji to order him and he would have accepted this union as the voice of God. So, what am I missing?'

'What cult are you talking about? There is nothing like a cult. I am a *Bahubali*, and I knew about Saurav, that he is a great guy, and I got him here and then got him abducted. None of the tapes that you have recorded into our conversation would help you, as they would not find all these records in your crime tapes. The tapes would have found dust before you could use them.'

'How did you get Saurav to get over to Muzaffarpur, all the way from Bangalore? How did you charm him into complete submission? I have heard the message to him, and it was not as charming. I would never have taken a flight and reached the next very day. What did you do to him? What power did you have over him?'

'Well, nothing really. We had a normal conversation, and he got excited. I was happy he would come to my town, and it would be easy for me to get him to marry my daughter. By the way, my daughter is beautiful, so you do not blame me here. While he lost his first love in Radha, I gave him a curated piece of my heart, my lovely daughter. He saw reason, and he got blown away by her. I did not have to get him married under a rifle butt. He liked her instantly.'

'That much I feel you are correct. I think Saurav likes her, but he is in awe of your persona. Look at you, I mean, at your age, which would be like seventy, you still have a splendid physique, tall, lean, and muscular. By the way, what is this symbol on your chest? Why did you give this same tattoo to your son-in-law?'

'Hey come on, Rajiv. I have not given any tattoo to Saurav. He had it when he came to Muzaffarpur.'

'That is my point, Rajveer ji! How come two individuals of different locations and different ages, have the same tattoo at the same position on their chest? How come both have rather steep undulations on your physical being, like sharp cut marks on the entire body? You give yourself pain and he gives himself pain. You guys are either soulmates from a different age or there is a better explanation. I found your symbol on a Brazilian website. You guys are members of a powerful cult which has members globally and you do anything in your power to protect the cult and its people. Are you not part of a powerful sect of people working under the religious and not so-religious beliefs of a madman, of a *guruji* (spiritual teacher) who is drunk on power and on pelf? Who is this madman, after all?'

'Enough. One more word against my *guruji* and you would bite dust right now! I would kill you right here and right now.'

Suddenly, Rajveer got up and ran into Rajiv with great force. He hit Rajiv's stomach with his bullhead. Rajiv went down hard on the ground, biting dust literally. He was in agony and by the time some constables ran towards them, Rajveer spat on Rajiv's face mouthing cuss words.

'How can you talk about an enlightened man in this language? I will kill you. You have bitten dust, by the grace of my *guruji*. I know how to kill you and still get out of here. Just look at me!' Rajveer shouted at the top of his voice, and he suddenly fell on the floor as he was hit on the head by a constable's lathi (baton).

Rajiv groaned but slowly got up. He looked in deep pain, but he had a smile on his face. He knew there was a *guruji* behind all of them. Dr. Tiru was correct in his prophesy.

Having gulped a cup of coffee, Rajiv got up on his feet once again. He knew he had limited time against such goons, so he had to do what he had to do, but fast.

'Saurav, why did you go running to this madman, Rajveer? What got you here? His daughter? I know for a fact that you were unaware he had a beautiful daughter and that he wanted her to marry you. I know you came for a different reason. I have booked you under multiple sections of the Indian Penal Code and you would never see the light of the day. So, if you want mercy, speak up and now is the only time. Even your mad father-in-law has spoken about your *guruji*. You do not have a chance left. He might be freed because he has agreed to become a state informer. What about you? Why did you commit this horrendous act of getting your first love, Radha murdered? Why did you send her photograph to those people in Netarhat? How did you gain by her inhuman death? You would not get place in hell, Saurav!'

Saurav was crying all this while, initially softly but slowly with Rajiv's lecture, he started crying loudly. He spoke incoherently, while crying.

'I have not killed Radha. I did not pass that kill judgement on her name. I did not even know that *guruji* had ordered her murder, rather sacrifice to the Almighty, for greater good. I got to know about it later, much later, when my fellow colleagues in the cult told me about his big heart and how he protected my soul. I loved Radha and I had lost her, so in my Guruji's logic, she should not have been anybody's. The only place reserved for her was in hell as she had chosen someone else, over his disciple. Had he told me about his step, prior to taking the step, I would still have gone with his decision. I was in awe of his powers, and he is powerful. He is a great man. He is a saint who would get the earth under his influence. Already our cult is now present in seventy-nine countries. We would take over the globe with the powers bestowed on us by our *guruji*. You have no idea he would get us out of here and you would not be able to book us for any crime. In fact, I have not committed any crime. I was unaware any such crime was being committed. *Guruji* was protecting me by not telling me about his decision on sacrificing Radha.

He knew, because of her sacrifice, our cult would grow to over a hundred countries soon. It is already happening. We are getting interested people talking in multiple countries across the world. It is the biggest secret society, and you are but a speck of dust in front of the cult juggernaut. Save yourself before they make you bite dust for eternity. Be gone, gentle soul and do not get in our way. I am a married man and I have not wronged anyone, so allow me to go to my family. I would go to Ranchi soon and get my parents to meet my wife. I would also like to go to Radha's house and pay my respects to her parents.'

'If your *guruji* is so powerful, why does he not appear on television and have a chat with me on prime-time. I would see who has more knowledge and who is superior overall in his intellect. I know, he must be a demagogue and a good speaker. He mesmerises you by the gift of his gab, does he not? Who is your *guruji*, challenge him from my side and I would see how he bites dust literally and figuratively?'

'Oh, you are someone who does not know his fury. I feel for you Rajiv, I truly feel for you. You would face a painful death, right as per our tradition. He would give you a thousand cuts, like our neighbours keep giving our country. Yes, a thousand cuts and you would bleed a slow death. All power would be sucked and drained out of your body and your spirit would squirm to see your bodily pain. It would leave a scar on your mind and on your soul. Be gone, gentle soul, be gone!'

'Your *guruji* is a murderer, and I am sure he would be a mass murderer. He would have ordered such kills, many times in the past. Why did you come over to Muzaffarpur? Tell me that, pretty boy?'

'I thought *guruji* wanted me to run some errand for him and I got his message through a fellow colleague, in fact through a commander in the hierarchy. Rajveer ji is many steps senior to me in the hierarchy. His wish was my command, and I ran to meet him, waiting for his orders. He ordered me to marry his daughter and I could not say no to it. She is a genuinely good person and beautiful too!' Saurav had a glint in his eyes and

Rajiv knew the girl had already become a pivot of his life.

'Yes, I know, she is beautiful but how come your *guruji* did not ask her to be a muse in his harem. I am sure he would have a harem like the old *sultans* (royals), am I right? Your wife could end up in his harem if he were to see her?' Rajiv smirked at Saurav.

'You do not know anything Rajiv. Our *guruji* is a gentle person. He does not do anything without a reason. Even if he has taken a few women in his family, it is only because they had to be liberated from their ordinary and painful lives. He has given them a beautiful life and he keeps them well. He is a powerful man. He is powerful externally as well as in his mind. People bow in his presence. I have seen ministers and other politicians bow in his presence. He is divine. Do not mess with him, else you are gone. He would get you thrown to Andamans, and you would never find your home back. Do not mess with us, here.'

'Saurav, I do not have anything against you. I need just two answers from you. Why did you get Radha killed? And what is this cult that you and your father-in-law represent? Why do you give yourself so much pain? Does it bring you salvation from your sins? Is that what your *guruji* tells you? Does he help you get salvation because you have to dirty your hands as he has several dirty tricks up his sleeves?'

'Hey come on, Inspector! I know you do not want any answers from me. I think you want to just put me behind bars for Radha's murder. Try it out because I can guarantee your case would be thrown out of the lower courts and you would not stand a chance. You do not have anything against me. Now, allow us to go or you are going to face music from unknown quarters. Do not be surprised if you see this place blown up. They would get us out well-nigh before you realise. No prison in India is secure and you must realise that.'

'I am letting you go. You can go wherever you want, Saurav. I would hold your father-in-law for a few days. I am still not done with my queries here. You need to come and meet me here, everyday over the next few days. Now, go!'

I had a plan and while his other colleagues were curious, he got into a jeep with a few of them and asked the driver to follow Saurav from a distance. Saurav had got into an auto and the police jeep was following him, keeping a safe distance. They saw Saurav crawl out of the auto and get into a rickshaw a couple of minutes later. He was trying to put someone off trail, and that might be the police. I was methodical on purpose. It was going to be difficult to get me off one's back. Saurav's rickshaw was stopped by a crashing Tata Sumo and before Saurav could realise, he was once again taken. This time not in a truck but an SUV which had almost black windowpanes.

I instructed my driver to follow the SUV, keeping a distance. We saw the SUV get into a narrow lane and then stop in the alley, blocking all traffic in the lane. By the time I could have asked my driver to stop his jeep, the jeep also got into the alley. I understood it was a trap and I asked the driver to hurriedly take the jeep backwards, out of the lane. Before the driver could, we had a barrage of gunfire from the SUV and from someone's roof.

Somehow, the jeep was taken back, out of the alley, all this while I and my team were ducking rather than firing ourselves. We knew we were outnumbered and outgunned. We did not have a choice. Thankfully, there were no casualties. I sent an SOS to the local police and to the state headquarters of the police force. I knew it was a dead alley and the criminals were also trapped. I asked for armed police and paramilitary police, with their gear. It was going to be a fight to the finish. I knew, we would get our answers there.

Soon enough, the local press and police along with an ambulance arrived. I was marshalling my resources. The local police DIG also arrived with his men. He was grades senior, so I had to work under his direction. The DIG understood my plan to approach the tallest building in the alley and take control of its roof. That would give us an advantage. We knew there were a lot of residents in that alley, and they should not be part of the collateral damage. Loudspeakers started blaring and the police could see residents running out of the alley, into the main road. Police had barricaded that entire area and all the residents were being taken to safety. Paramilitary troops in riot gear were deployed to keep the alley safe. Some of our men had already climbed onto and behind the boundary walls of the buildings and a couple of them were now stationed on the roof with big guns in their hands. They were all focused on the activity in a particular building, in front of which the Sumo was parked. It was evening time, and the episode was being telecast live on all news channels in the states of Jharkhand and Bihar, while the national channels were also reporting from the location. I knew we had an upper hand as *guruji* had been taken this misstep of putting us under fire inside the town. With the kind of resources, we had marshalled, it was going to be easy for us and he was going to be a loser.

I had also worn a helmet and a bullet proof gear. I roared on the loudspeaker, like a lion calling out its prey. The entire place was silent. I was a bit annoyed and a little disturbed. I felt I was roaring in an empty jungle and my prey had already left the area. I gave the order to charge, taking approval from the DIG. Policemen entered the building swiftly, nullifying any advantage that the criminals might have.

They ran up the building, looking at every corner of the same, but they could not find anyone there. They found only a senior citizen, who was lying in his bed, and he was someone who could not move an inch due to his medical condition.

They asked the man about the whereabouts of the criminals, and they realised they went out from one roof to the other, utilising the proximity of all the buildings in the area. By the time the police had reached the building, these people could have been anywhere, in fact they might even be just behind the police barricade, looking at police action.

It was a major embarrassment for me and my team. The DIG admonished me for my planning and went away. I was left to answer the media. That I did with great courage and confidence as I was already passionate about the case and the press was now on my side. They knew I was onto something big. They felt I was after some important people, who could be *bahubalis* or politicians. I announced that we were close to a major victory against a major cult and that we might even be killed as many senior functionaries as possible in the bureaucracy and ministry were involved. Radha's case was not that of a lady alone, it was to bring down an empire built on false religious undertones, faith, and belief.

I knew I was near, and I would find a way to reach out to Saurav again. I knew it was important to get back to his father-in-law and he must be well guarded. That evening was important, and I decided to stay back at the thana that night.

I got a call from my senior at Lohardaga who asked me to stay sharp. He also advised me to keep a large team of police constables at the thana that night. I had my plan ready, and I ordered some food for all the policemen in the thana. I requested the thana in charge to stay in the premises and not to go back home. He said he believed there would be a break-out attempt that night.

Policemen were tense and they had double checked their weapons, kept it clean and checked their cartridges. They expected the criminals to have better firepower than them, but they knew, with passionate officers around them, they were in good company. I had taken over the management of the thana premises that night and I had posted two constables on the roof. Whilst they were connected on a walkie, I got jammers installed in the area. So, cell phone connections were not there for people to converse. I wanted everyone to stay sharp and I utilised the team to change duties every half an hour. I kept them charged and I kept an eye outside in the area. There were two ways to reach the thana, that was in a residential area. I had kept a small police picket on either side, so that they could tackle them there itself and neutralise the threat. Even if they could not neutralise the threat, we would know of an impending threat, and we would get into action.

Rajveer made a mockery of me in his acerbic style and challenged me to keep him for the night. He believed his friends would come and whisk him away in the darkness of the night and the police would be left in shame and denial.

I knew it was an important event in my life and I had to keep my calm and hold my nerves. I knew the policemen were fierce, if motivated properly, even with their archaic arms and ammunitions. I was there with all of them, waiting for an impending attack, ferocious like a lioness looking to protect her cubs. I was motivated and I had reasons to be on a high alert. My grey matter was helping me deconstruct the events of the last few days and I felt the attack would happen in the wee hours of the morning.

CHAPTER 31

17 March 2010: 03:00 Hrs

I felt restless and sleepy. I got up again and marched up and down the thana to keep my sanity and to talk to policemen also and help them get out of their slumber.

The entire area was quiet, like it was before a storm. Only the cracking sound of walkies broke the silence erratically. Suddenly, I picked up a commentary from the west side pocket. They said two Tama Sumo had broken the barricades, and they were moving towards our police station. The policemen had challenged them and fired at them, but they just moved ahead, with no care in the Goddamn world.

I got everyone ready and charged up. I asked the west and the east side picket policemen to move towards the police station and try to neutralize them before they enter the station. The station gates were closed, and we jammed the doors with enough furniture and barricades we could lay our hands on. I left nothing to chance as I knew those criminals will be loaded to the teeth and their firepower would be Light Machine Guns and what not. Policemen had their rifles that could fire a couple of rounds and revolvers with six rounds of fire.

I informed the constables on the roof to be vigilant and to fire at the two Sumos as soon as they came in range. I went to the cell where we had kept Rajveer and I kicked him in his face with all my might. I showed my frustration, and I knew I was better than this. Rajveer shouted the filthiest of cuss words, but I just stormed out of his cell. I had to protect my police team. I called out the DIG for help and asked for the paramilitary troops to be sent immediately for backup.

The two Sumos came in front of the thana, and a gun-toting guy came out of the sunroof and neutralized the constables on the roof with a sudden burst of shells. It was swift and ample.

I asked the team in the front area to keep themselves safe while firing at the SUVs. The SUVs had bulletproof glass, and it absorbed the firepower coming in from the west and the east picket policemen. They were also getting some rounds directly from within the thana.

I was told by the paramilitary troops they were just twenty minutes out and that we should keep the criminals at bay for at least that time. Before I could think of anything, they fired a mortar from within the SUV and it took away the front gate, the door and a portion of the roof of the station. The policemen who were in front, holding the fort for the thana, were all but dead in an instant. The sound of the rocket had ripped that area of its deep sleep and people started getting up and putting their lights on. People in the area could watch the police and the criminal gang fight, and it was crazy. The action was swift and with an unimaginable force. I prepared us to take on the might of local gangsters while the team that came was possibly full of international war criminals. They were there with a defined purpose to kill anyone that came in their way and they had to take away Rajveer as a trophy. The criminals had far higher firepower, and they just zoomed in and zoomed out of the thana precincts, hurting everyone on their way and taking away Rajveer. I also received a bullet wound on my left arm, in my biceps. The bullet had just grazed my arm, but it was painful.

Policemen had no time to react, and they outgunned and outwit us. I could not fathom what just happened and we should have kept Central Reserve Police Force (CRPF) battalion from the beginning. We were under prepared but by this action, *guruji* had brought out the war in the open and the state could not hide anymore. They had to act, and they could not just leave it up to me to take care. It had surprised the common man, and they demanded action against the criminals. They wanted my protection. It was on a loop on various television channels, including the national media.

I was not someone who would take defeat easily. I knew the common man would force my seniors to allocate adequate resources for this major lapse in internal security. I knew my time would come, and I had all but lost a battle within a war. I knew I would take the war to the enemy's door, and soon.

There was a massive commotion, and the entire top brass of the local police were there within the hour. Paramilitary forces had arrived, and they helped clear the rubble and take away the bodies. A few policemen had survived, and we sent them to the nearby hospitals. It was a devastating day for the police, and I was pensive and morose. I had lost many policemen, and it was something that gave the required strength to my conviction. My counterpart of the police station was also badly injured, and he was hospitalized. I had decided not to leave those goons, and I knew I would go after *guruji* with double strength.

I spoke to the media, and I showed my resolve to go after the mighty people. I was sorry for losing lives of my fellow policemen, and I said it was necessary to take down the mafia as it was way too big and way too powerful. It was not good for my state or for my country, and they had to face justice. People of the country rallied behind me, as did the media.

In an interview the same evening, the Bihar state police chief announced he had spoken to the Jharkhand police chief, and I was being appointed as the in-charge of the investigations. They had formed a joint task force under my leadership, having men from both the Jharkhand and the Bihar police teams.

The Bihar state police chief also announced the team had his full support and we would not find ourselves wanting the next time such a police action took place.

I had a carte blanche, and I knew it was for real, but for a brief period. Such task forces cannot work beyond a certain period, and I had to do everything I had learnt to get back in business.

I had kept a team of my finest policemen outside Rajveer's mansion. Rajveer's house and office phones were being tapped and his mobiles were not in use anymore. Saurav's mobile was also unreachable for most parts. The chase had become tricky, but I had to think of something that would give away the criminals.

I enjoyed being in Muzaffarpur, over Latehar and while I wanted to wrap up the investigation for good, I did not want to go back to Latehar. Was there anything left for me there? Diya was obviously involved in this case and a honey trap. Her phone had gone silent. I could not reach it. Her sim card had been destroyed. I would never find her. She should not have done this to me. For me, it was almost as if it was my first love. I had liked her quite a lot and while I used to think I knew little about her; it was difficult to let go. She wasn't from Latehar, of which I had little doubt. I had sent Pradeep to the house she had shown me as her home. We got to know she was a Paying Guest there. We got her documents checked, and it was all forged. So, in my best estimates, during this investigation, I could find her out as well. She must be close to guruji, for being used in the manner that she had been used. She might be a part of his harem. I felt icky about it. I was not happy a woman had used me and thrown me out of her life for good. To her, I was only a source of first-hand information while I was trying to create my life with her. Small mercies, thy Lordship!

CHAPTER 32

19 March 2010: 13:00 Hrs & 20 March 11:00 Hrs

I met my entire task force team and gave them instructions. I asked them to loop me in if they heard anything from the people who were being tapped. I also wanted my policemen to get creative and get me as much information as possible about Radha, Ravi and Saurav. I knew there was something not right and the answers might come from their past. I asked the policemen to track their profiles on Facebook and other social media accounts.

Policemen collated data about all the people involved in the said crime, from as many angles as possible. There were side-by-side interviews happening, like Bholu's wife had been interviewed twice. A policeman had gone to Mumbai to meet Akshay and his parents, and he interviewed them thoroughly. Similarly, policemen at Ranchi had interviewed Saurav's parents, and they had monitored their movements.

Ravi's social media accounts and his bank and other details were mapped and were being kept track of. Policemen were doing their job with diligence, and they were committed to find the culprits and take charge of the situation. They wanted to avenge multiple deaths of policemen at the hands of the criminals, and they were in no mood to get deflected from their duties. It had become personal, and they were doing all it takes to find Rajveer and Saurav.

'Sir, we have found Saurav. He has accessed his Facebook account a moment back, and he is in Patna. We know his exact location, but we do not know whether he is alone or he is with Rajveer. They are in Kankarbagh area, in a residential colony. What should we do now? We think he was trying to connect with someone online, but he might have realized we will track him. Hence, he logged off within a couple of minutes. That was sufficient time for us to track him, as we were monitoring his profile. What should we do now?'

'Let a few of us go to Patna. I will inform the local station in-charge to organize a team of policemen. We would raid the area together, within 5 pm. We leave in ten minutes. Do not inform anyone of anything yet. I will inform whoever I wish to. I do not want any word going out and Saurav panicking again. Let us stay our course and we will nab him today before the end of day.'

It was a battle to avenge the martyrs, and I accorded it supreme priority. This time, we were better prepared. I asked for a CRPF unit to follow us to Patna. We had enough firepower to field even fifty goons that day. If only we were better prepared the other day, it would have saved so many of us. I was fully responsible for so many lives and I had not kept my word to them. I had faltered. I could not gauge the strength of the opponent. This had been a blunder, and it showed in those many deaths of policemen. It had never happened in the past, within the police station premises, in a city. I did not feel well, and I felt guilty about war crimes. I had not done enough. I also had a survivor's guilt. I knew it would not allow me to sleep for months to come.

We reached the location at around 4.45 pm. We did not have any time to waste. I got two snipers installed in the nearby rooftops. We had left our vehicles a few metres away. Soldiers were on foot, and they were raring to go. I had told everyone that I needed Saurav alive, and we had to arrest him. Nearby camera and cellphone toting people were covering the police action on videos that went viral within no time. Our snipers confirmed Saurav's presence in the dining area. He was having tea. They did not find any gunmen inside. The house must have been mostly empty, other than one woman who was serving Saurav.

In a swift action, we apprehended Saurav. The media had already come over in their large vans and they covered it widely. We took Saurav back to Muzaffarpur the same evening. Rajveer was not there with Saurav and Saurav was clueless about his whereabouts. Police got cracking on the ownership papers of the house where Saurav had been kept. It was a house on rent and the flat owner had no clue they had kept Saurav. They took the rent in the name of some Mr. Das and the flat owner used to get his rent in his account within the 7th instant, every month. He was, therefore, not bothered by who stayed there. Mr. Das was not available for police questioning. He was absconding.

14 March 2010: 11:00 Hrs

'Sir, there was a call to Ravi today, a while back. Someone again asked him if he was okay and if his friend was ok. To that, Ravi did not respond, and he kept the phone. He has himself tried to connect with Saurav multiple times over, but to no avail. I thought I should report to you about this phone call, although there is nothing there for us.' Police constable stated.

'Um, er… wait. Okay, you go. Let me have a chat with Ravi. I have his mobile number.' Rajiv stated.

'Ravi, this is Rajiv. Hope you remember me?'

'Yes, Inspector Rajiv. How can I forget about you? Ever since Radha's ghastly murder, we have never had any good fortune. First, it was Radha. Now I think even Saurav is in trouble, although I do not think he was involved in her murder.' Ravi blurted out.

'Ravi, how can you say that?'

'Rajiv ji, I know Saurav and deep down, I can say, he is a good boy. He is in trouble and therefore he has done whatever he has done. I have been reading the progress of this case and I know you have not found Saurav's blood there in Netarhat, among others, while you found Akshay's blood. Had you found Saurav's blood, he would have been in your custody. Also, he used to ike Radha, if not love her with the same intensity that Radha loved him. At least that was his stated position. However, to my mind, Saurav used to love Radha more than Radha could see and he had Radha for the taking. He did not move forward with the many subtle hints that Radha gave him. I can tell you Radha would have been thrilled to marry

Saurav, but for his own obstinacy or slow reaction to her proposal. I could have married Radha, but for her height. She used to like me a lot and even I used to like her. However, in my scheme of things, our marriage would not have worked out, as she was taller than me and smarter.

I want my wife to be not more than my height, even if she is very tall.'

'That proves nothing, Ravi. Yes, I know both of you liked Radha, and she liked both of you. That changes nothing. A new guy took her, having impressed her within a month of his getting back into her life after college. He blew her off her feet and both of you kept sulking. I would say, both of you have had a grudge against Akshay and it directly involved you guys, in this case. You have taken the benefit of knowing about this cult, and both of you are members of the same. So, let me tell you, I have sent a police team to your house, and they would be at your front door any minute now. Do not run away as they would still catch you and try you for Radha's cold-blooded murder.'

'What are you saying, Inspector? This is all rubbish and you know it well enough. I do not fear your ways, as I am not involved in this case at all. My conscience is clear and I hold my head high.' Saying thus, Ravi kept the phone. He rang up someone and told him, 'I am in trouble. Get me. Fools are on their way and would be here any minute.'

'Hang in there or maybe just go out of the house and stay around the corner building. My guy would pick you up within twenty minutes. Keep away from police jeeps, etc. Now, go!'

Ravi was not aware we had bugged his entire house during our last raid. We could hear all his conversations.

I knew Ravi would do something as naïve as this. I had a feeling he would lead us directly to the cult members. It would be easy to take them down, away from Muzaffarpur, in a new location, where they might not be having a similar firepower. It was our chance, and I had good vibes about the same. I knew we had to keep this under wraps for a bit, and that we needed swift police action.

I had become wary ever since the blow on the back of my head. It was Diya, perhaps. She might have wanted to keep her identity a secret from me, so the blow. However, she obviously did not wish to kill me then. She might not have had her orders to that effect. So, it was a deflection tactic and nothing more.

They took Ravi to a suburban area in Bangalore and taken inside an old hotel that was otherwise closed for tourists. My team had followed the SUV to that location. I asked them to monitor the hotel but not to enter at all. I had asked the policemen to be in plain clothes and not to make themselves seen in the area.

Ravi had already switched off his mobile phone and was unavailable to the world.

They informed me that Ravi was being taken to the Bangalore airport. I spoke to the airport police, and I instructed them to inform me of Ravi's destination. The airport authorities informed me that Ravi was traveling to Mumbai on a Jet Airways flight, and he had a further ticket to London. Ravi would check into the international flight only at Mumbai.

I informed the Mumbai police to apprehend Ravi at Mumbai airport as soon as he checked into the London flight.

I had monitored the developing situation throughout the day. Two policemen took Ravi and the other two people to Patna on the next available flight. I was at the Patna airport to welcome them.

As soon as they reached the circuit house, where I wanted to house them for the evening, I tore off Ravi's shirt in a jiffy before Ravi could realize. In another instant, he tore off the shirt of the other people accompanying Ravi.

I stunned them by my sudden action. Ravi and the other two people had sharp cuts all over their upper body, and they had a tattoo of an eagle which had a dagger to her eye and a drop of blood was oozing out of the same.

I wanted answers. I knew I would be in deep trouble, as I had three members of the cult with me that evening. I had only two constables with me. *Guruji* could organize a similar action to free their cult members. I moved Ravi and the other two cult members to the Beur Central Jail at Patna. I spoke to the Jailor-in-charge and they organized safe room for the three new prisoners.

I knew that the three of them had to be produced in front of a magistrate the next morning and there could be an attack while they were on the road to the court. I spoke to his superiors and informed them of his predicament. They gave their support, and I created a defensive traffic movement for the next morning. He had pinch-hitters in three similar looking police vans. No one knew which van housed the three criminals.

The passage to the court was event-free, and the judge handed over the three prisoners to the state police on a fourteen-day remand for further investigation.

I was in the front van while returning to Beur Central Jail and I kept an eye out for any major movement of large vehicles. I had organized trucks to be kept out of that area for at least two hours. I asked the local traffic police to keep looking for multiple Sumo SUVs, with dark tinted glasses, and to report immediately.

I heard on the walkie-talkie about an instance of a couple of SUVs moving towards the Central Jail. I asked the Jailer to keep the gates of the Central Jail open and to have a good police presence at the entrance. I informed the Jailer I was five minutes out. I also despatched a CRPF helicopter to cover the policemen at Beur Central Jail.

Before the Jailer could organize a decent police presence at the entrance of the jail, and before the helicopter could reach the location, three SUVs came in from different directions and they opened fire at the jail entrance. The jail guards ran for cover, and they shut the jail entrance door from inside. That gave enough time for the Sumo guys to cement their position at the jail gate, and they waited for the prison vans to get there. I heard of this commotion at the precincts of the jail, so I tried diverting the three vans that were carrying Ravi and team. However, we were late, and we had almost reached the jail. Our vehicles were spotted, and these men with AK-47 guns followed us, opening fire indiscriminately. It was within minutes that a huge blowout operation happened. The Sumo guys used massive force using AK-47 rifles. Police rifles were no match. In a swift operation, they got hold of the three prisoners and whisked them away, in front of me and my team of almost twenty police officials. They had taken care not to kill policemen this time around. They went to scare the policemen, and they carried out their breakout operation successfully.

I felt disappointed at not being able to hold Ravi any longer. He might have given us a clue or two. The police were looking inefficient in front of the world at large, and the breakout scene was being played out on television screens. Some channels had already started showing the events till date and it only showed the state police as inept.

Later, at a media hearing, I looked dazed and thoughtful. While my senior was speaking to the media, I suddenly came towards the microphone and told my superior to announce we had enough clues to nab the culprits.

The journalists asked me multiple questions, and I took them with elan. I announced I had the culprits, and I would nab them in an operation the same night. It was going to be the last operation, and my team would nab all the major culprits. I suggested we would use the Rapid Action Force (RAF) along with the CRPF in the raid that I would conduct within the hour.

There was a lot of commotion, and I went out with my superior. I wanted my superior to cover for me during the operation. I also wanted my superior not to allow anyone else to get in touch with me over the next couple of hours. I told him to just say that Rajiv was unreachable, and his entire team had left their walkies and mobiles in the local station.

I used a jammer to jam the mobile phones of all the constables in my unit and of all the soldiers from RAF and CRPF. We went to an outskirt's location, near Danapur. We reached the exact location where they had kept Ravi and the other two criminals. While getting these criminals from the court, I had planted all of them with trackers. All the trackers were showing in the same room, inside the small building. This building was the lone building in that area and away from a cluster of houses in the locality.

We parked our vans a little distance away, and I asked a couple of men to study the location for any movements. They came back saying they could see armed guards in the house, and it had at least twenty guards. The house had a barbed wire fencing, and it might have electricity running on the wire. The area was pitch dark otherwise, and they needed to have enough lights around.

I thought of testing the guards, and I got one van to send high luminosity through a torch gun. There was frantic activity in the house and suddenly firing started from within the house. Policemen ducked for cover, and I advised them to go in from all four sides, while keeping the light switched on only from one direction. They could see there was a massive build-up of gunmen towards the front side of the house. My instructions were explicit to the policemen, to the CRPF and to the RAF team, not to maim or kill any inmate. I wanted Ravi and the other two guys alive. This was my last resort, and I had to unravel the mystery. It was important to nab the culprits and get them to narrate the story.

I was standing towards the frontal location from where we had put a high-intensity light towards the building. We had taken cover behind the rocky surface and behind our trucks. I was connected to all my team members by walkies, and I was giving them instruction. All the three teams of seven members each had reached the house from back and from the two sides. I asked the guys to test whether they had electrified the fence. To our great surprise, it was not. It was easy to just cut the fence and enter the compound. It was a big bungalow, and the land was quite large. I asked the guys to cut the fence for two people to enter together. My team did the fence-cutting work on all three sides. We were constantly under fire, and we knew we had little time, as they would soon get backup teams coming their way.

We had to get in swiftly and neutralize the guards, get our booty and walk away. We had a maximum of five minutes to complete the operation, as per my calculations. I asked the teams on the three sides to take out any guards on their sides before entering the compound. I also asked at least one person from each side to just run towards the bungalow and enter without waiting to neutralize the guards. We coordinated our stop watches, and I gave them exactly three minutes to bring out Ravi and the other two guys. I was watching as I started getting updates from the three teams. In the first one minute, at least five guards were neutralized. I was tense but happy that my team was working with laser focused precision. They continued to take out those guards, including the few who were on the front side, spraying bullets on us. They did not realize we could attack them from all directions. We had the surprise element in our favor and before they could figure out; the operation had almost ended. Three of my people confirmed having reached the room where Ravi and team were. They had taken out two guards while getting into the bungalow. Within three minutes, the operation ended. I went inside to see a terrorized group of people, among others, Ravi and the two other guys, were also there. I could see a few other people inside. My jaw widened to see the police chief of the state there. He was a culprit, as it looked. Beside him, I saw Diya, who had a puzzled and terrorized look on her face. For a fleeting moment, I became nervous and ready to take Diya in my arms. Better sense prevailed, and I asked my team to apprehend her along with the others. She did not look like a hardened criminal, and possibly she was carrying out the orders of *guruji*, as a disciple, brought together by faith. I could not have discussed her predicament at that hour.

The police chief of Bihar tried to take over the proceedings from me, talking me out of his problems, but I was in no mood to listen. He said he had got a wind of these culprits and he had inserted himself as an agent, to figure out how to destroy the cult. His stories made no sense, and I was not a juvenile. I instructed my team to take all the culprits to the vans. I had also got a unit of journalists from some television channels with me, and we paraded the inmates in front of the media.

Ravi and the two cult members, along with the state police chief, and the first lady in my life, Diya, were in the RAF van, and we were on our way back to Beur Central Jail.

I informed my superior about our swift action and that we were getting back to the city. I was in the van with the three cult members, the state DGP, and Diya, and I was trying to talk to Ravi. Our van was in the middle. We had a police jeep in front. Before we would have gone even five minutes towards Patna, there was a loud boom. The police jeep in front went up in flames. A rocket hit it. Our van also halted, and I got the five prisoners out of the van. We ran towards safety, but we soon saw our vehicle also going up in the air in a loud boom, falling back on the road in a loud bang. The vehicles were in a fireball. Most of my team was safe, but the constables in the police jeep might not have been so lucky. We took our positions on the roadside and we came under heavy fire. This time, however, we had RAF and CRPF teams, apart from my policemen. I told my policemen to run for cover as they could not have fought a pitched battle against this heavily loaded enemy. RAF and CRPF teams had massive firepower themselves. They started taking out the enemy by spraying them with bullets and grenades. Never earlier had a pitched battle been fought on the roads of Patna and we were creating history daily now. Guruji had gone too far, and he had to be apprehended. I asked my men to take a full video of the proceedings. The three prisoners were with me, on the roadside, safely behind three rows of policemen, RAF and CRPF team members. They would obviously take out guards on their way. It took us almost twenty minutes of intense battle to defeat the enemy. We lost at least eight men while the opponent lost all its men in this operation. We saw at least twenty-two bodies lying in the area. I had already transmitted an SOS to my superior, and we soon got air support and ground support. I went in the helicopter with the prisoners and deposited them in Beur Central Jail.

Within minutes, the news went viral that it also involved the police chief in this entire mess, and he was the culprit. I had already seen the tattoo on the skin of the police chief, and I knew it was only the beginning.

It was a major event in the case, and it changed the fortunes of the state. Over the next few days, they conducted a lot of raids at different parts of the country and they apprehended cult members. They left it to me to figure out which all members were involved in various cases of loot and murder in the past and who all needed to be apprehended for their actions of omission and commission.

I found a red diary with the names of all members of the secret society and their local police were informed about their whereabouts. The diary also mentioned the major mafia actions undertaken by the cult and the members of the cult that were involved in those crimes.

As it always happens, some of these powerful people went underground and they would continue to haunt the police in the future.

I had become an overnight star and people looked forward to getting to know about my future exploits. All my cases were always in a limelight and there was a media frenzy around it. Journalists just did their job of keeping me as a star and as a savior for the departments' name and news items around me, the star detective would get lapped up by the masses. I had become a celebrity, but I continued to be grounded in my approach, methodical by nature and sharp by design.

While this is a prequel to the series The Kanke Killings Trilogy, which had Two Indian Girls as the debut novel, Fatal Belief as the second in series, and Daybreak as the third and the last novel of the trilogy. I as time the narrator, I also do not know whether the storyteller that I am, would I ever get back with a sequel to this trilogy. This problem confounds my present, but I would find a solution to it by the time you would have read the four novels already out there.

Read Two Indian Girls here: https://bklnk.com/B094XBGD1G

Also read the Epilogue below.

EPILOGUE

28 May 2010: 13:00 Hrs
I was with Radha's parents at their house. They were ever so grateful, and they had expressed their gratitude to me in no uncertain terms. They had found a closure in the sensational case that started with an unfortunate case of Radha's murder and ended up occupying the prime time of national television channels over the next couple of months.

I requested the two states of Bihar and Jharkhand for some time to be posted at Patna, as I wanted to work in the state for a while and help fight some major crimes in the area. Jharkhand was peaceful, and I had little to do there, other than the usual operations against the Naxalites.

The two state governments agreed to my request, and they gave me a posting at Patna.

Radha's murderer was the existing *Guruji* of the cult. The cult used to anoint a new *Guruji* every few years, and they were always powerful people of the sect. They were typically senior bureaucrats or senior politicians who could wield enough state power, and they would use it to the maximum to create a larger sect. They would not undertake multiple criminal activities, but they had to protect the secrecy of the cult with their lives. The *Adi-Guru*, as the followers used to call it, was the first Guru who started the cult, centuries before Christ.

The cult-members believed the *Adi-Guru* was an ascetic who used to be in *sadhana* (deep and prolonged prayers) for days together. He used to stay in the jungles, and he was fond of snakes. He used to go into his sadhana by preparing his body. He used to give himself sharp cuts and then he would lie on the ground, naked and get into deep prayers for multiple days. It is said that snakes used to guard him during his routine prayer sessions and ward off any evil.

In one such *sadhana*, the Adi-Guru flushed a dagger in his hand while in prayers, with his eyes closed and used it with an unseen speed. The dagger went through the right eye of the eagle, to his left eye, killing the eagle in an instant. He later got up and realized he had killed an eagle while in his prayers and it was only to ward off the eagle from taking away one of his special snakes.

Ever since, the local people in that area started calling him the snake God or the *Adi-Guru*. His fame grew, and he took many disciples. It is said that the same cult grew into a large secret society, and it has members across multiple nations. One erstwhile Guruji gave it the name, the Snake Charmers cult. I and my team had sent out special teams to work on getting all the culprits to book. We booked all of them under multiple sections of the IPC including section 120B, for the overall conspiracy. Not all members were touched.

It is not a crime to be a part of a secret society. However, if any member got involved in any crime, being a member of the society, we could book them under the laws of the land, for hatching the conspiracy.

Media discussed Radha's case threadbare. She fell prey to a megalomaniac in the state police chief, who was the *Guruji* of the sect. He used to like Saurav and Ravi personally and he found it unpalatable to accept that Radha would marry someone else. Ravi himself was not okay with Radha marrying Akshay, and he had discussed the issue with his *Guruji* in one communion. *Guruji* did not speak to Saurav about it, but he gave the kill order, so that the pride of Saurav could be kept and he did not feel bad about Radha's marriage to Akshay.

As Saurav was unaware of the conspiracy around Radha's murder, the courts set him free, and he went to his house at Ranchi with his wife. He had grown fond of his wife and while he could have left her; he did not want to. She might have come to him in his life by force, but he wanted to have her in his life.

Ravi was apprehended and found a conspirator in the crime. His life, as we know, was over. All major members of the cult, including the police chief, were behind bars and they would all face justice soon.

It was tough time for Saurav's and Ravi's parents, but they handled it in their own ways. Akshay was sad to see Ravi's involvement, and he went over to meet Ravi in the prison. He shouted at Ravi, and he said he could not believe it was Ravi as he always knew the three musketeers were great together and the two boys were her guardians in the city.

Radha had fallen to her best friend and guardian's machinations against her. She could not even understand the ill-feelings in Ravi's minds for her and she might have wanted not to unravel the mystery herself, as the story was quite painful. Akshay was a broken man, and he felt truly agonized to have lost Radha to her best friends who were culprits. Saurav also felt bad for Radha, and he hated his best friend, Ravi. He could not even imagine Ravi could do something like this to Radha, for he knew Ravi also liked Radha as much as he liked her. He would always entertain the thought in his mind about why Ravi did what he did. It would require psychologists to find it out for him, and he depended on Inspector Rajiv.

Rajiv was a media celebrity, and he had taken a house on rent in the Boring Road area of Patna. The residents of Patna were happy they had a fighting fit officer in their midst and big criminals would fear him before committing any ghastly crime. The city folks welcomed Rajiv to the city.

LET'S CONNECT

15 November 2021

    I sincerely hope you enjoyed the book. I would love to know your feedback. A slight gesture of rating and reviewing it on Amazon, Goodreads, or your social media handles would provide a lot of comfort and happiness to your friend here.

    This story would develop, and new characters would get introduced, but I would like to know your opinion about some of the important characters in this novel. We had the feisty one and the sober one, and a word on that would help me understand your taste. We also had some fine police personnel in the two books that you read, including this one and Two Indian Girls earlier. Let me know your overall feedback on the developing story.

    I would love it if you connected with me here:

Instagram: https://instagram.com/authorkinshuk

Twitter: https://twitter.com/AuthorKinshuk

Facebook: https://facebook.com/AuthorKinshuk

BookBub: https://www.bookbub.com/profile/2611953880?

Goodreads: https://www.goodreads.com/user/show/37989238-kumar-kinshuk

YouTube: https://www.youtube.com/channel/UCsKUK-3DNTh116Y5B7wTdAA/featured

Email: authorkinshuk@kumarkinshuk.com

Website: https://kumarkinshuk.com

Blog: https://kumarkinshuk.com/blog/

THANK YOU

Printed in Great Britain
by Amazon